Praise for the Eagles and Dragons series...

Historic Novel Society:

"...Haviaras handles it all with smooth skill. The world of third-century Rome...is colourfully vivid here, and Haviaras manages to invest even his secondary and tertiary characters with believable, three-dimensional humanity."

Amazon Readers:

"Graphic, uncompromising and honest... A novel of heroic men and the truth of the uncompromising horror of close combat total war..."

"Raw and unswerving in war and peace... New author to me but ranks along side Ben Kane and Simon Scarrow. The attention to detail and all the gory details are inspiring and the author doesn't invite you into the book he drags you by the nasal hairs into the world of Roman life sweat, tears, blood, guts and sheer heroism. Well worth a night's reading because once started it's hard to put down."

"Historical fiction at its best! ... if you like your historical fiction to be an education as well as a fun read, this is the book for you!"

"Loved this book! I'm an avid fan of Ancient Rome and this story is, perhaps, one of the best I've ever read."

"An outstanding and compelling novel!"

"I would add this author to some of the great historical writers such as Conn Iggulden, Simon Scarrow and David Gemmell. The characters were described in such a way that it was easy to picture them as if they were real and have lived in the past, the book flowed with an ease that any reader, novice to advanced can enjoy and become fully immersed..."

"One in a series of tales which would rank them alongside Bernard Cornwell, Simon Scarrow, Robert Ludlum, James Boschert and others of their ilk. The story and character development and the pacing of the exciting military actions frankly are superb and edge of your seat! The historical environment and settings have been well researched to make the story lines so very believable!! I can hardly wait for what I hope will be many sequels! If you enjoy Roman historical fiction, you do not want to miss this series!"

Goodreads:

"... a very entertaining read; Haviaras has both a fluid writing style, and a good eye for historical detail, and explores in far more detail the faith of the average Roman than do most authors."

Kobo:

"I can't remember the last time that a book stirred so many emotions! I laughed, cried and cheered my way through this book and can't wait to meet again this wonderful family of characters. Roll on to the next book!"

Join the Legions!

Sign-up for the Eagles and Dragons Publishing
Newsletter and get a FREE BOOK today.

Subscribers get first access to new releases, special
offers, and much more.

Go to:
www.eaglesanddragonspublishing.com

For my mother, who taught me to believe…

Για τη μητέρα μου, που μου δίδαξε να έχω πίστη…

THE
STOLEN
THRONE

EAGLES AND DRAGONS

BOOK V

ADAM ALEXANDER HAVIARAS

PROLOGUS

Howling wind and the dead raced among the naked, black trees of a distant forest. There was fear among those shades that lingered there on that moonless night. They cowered behind trunk and boulder, their liquid eyes watching for her, that goddess of death, the dread queen of night.

Dull brown leaves crackled, and the cawing of ravens followed, heralding her arrival. Bare feet, pale as death, trod the forest floor, trailed by a torn black cloak.

She had arrived, and the dead knew it, but so did the living, for unbeknownst to them, the nightmares they had that night were the seedlings of her passing, the fears they felt, the horrors they imagined. All of them were hers.

She walked toward a green firelight in a clearing, and there she found her hunter, sitting erect before the flames, sharpening a long, black sword that had seen more than its fair share of blood on the hunt.

"You prepare for the Wild Hunt then?" her voice was icy, but did not bother him, for he knew her and she him, and so it had been for ages.

"Yes. Samhain approaches, and the hordes of the dead must ride through the world with havoc and fear."

"And so it is," she said, staring at him so intensely that his head turned quickly to meet her gaze. "You prey on the weak and vulnerable."

"Yes. As always," the hunter said.

"I have a prey for you that needs killing," she said.

"Oh?" he said, standing up, taller than her but radiating nowhere near the menace she had. He bowed to her. "What prey?"

"A dragon."

"I've slain dragons before, and tamed them."

"Not such as this," she said, her eyes looking up to the sharp, dark clouds in the night sky above. "I want him to suffer...I want him dead."

"When?"

"In time."

"Where?" he asked.

"I will let you know," she answered, her gaze insisting on silence.

The hunter felt a chill run the length of his strong body. "As you command, Morrigan."

"Yes."

In the treetops above, the silhouettes of a hundred ravens showed against the pale sky, as if already gathered for the gorging.

"Get to Dumnonia, and wait. There will you hunt," she said, her eyes closed as if seeing something from afar. "Go now!"

The hunter bowed to her and moved backward from the green flames of his fire to find his shadow horse. He leapt up and looked down at the dark goddess.

"I'll await your messengers," he said, before raising a hunting horn to his mouth and blowing. The sound shook the trees about them and sent the ravens to flight, and a moment later the hunter was riding away through the darkness of the woods, followed by three monstrous, black hounds.

The Morrigan watched him leave and smiled to herself, glad of the darkness wrapped about her.

"The time of death is near..."

I

DEBITUM

'The Debt'

October - A.D. 210

Summer was ended, and the cold, damp cling of autumn had spread over the expanses of southern Britannia as the month of October arrived. The one-time summer sky was now assaulted with sharp clouds which Boreas blew across the land. The rains had not started yet, but their windy herald had arrived to chill mornings and evenings in every home and villa estate.

The three horsemen had left the deep green embankments of the hillfort just after Apollo's light had cracked the distant horizon. They had passed through the southwestern gatehouse and followed the winding path down and around to join the Roman road to Lindinis where they would continue on the Fosse Way to Isca.

They had a long journey ahead.

Lucius Metellus Anguis reined in his dapple grey stallion, Lunaris, and turned to take a last look at the place that had become his family's home since his forced furlough from command.

His companions, Lucius' princeps and a Sarmatian king, Dagon, and the loyal Briton, Einion, son of Cunnomore, stopped a little past Lucius and waited as he stared at the distant hill.

Lucius felt the pull of the fortress, his family safe within the high green embankments where gnarled oak trees sprouted from the earth and crows dove in the sky above. He had not wanted to leave Adara and the children, not then, after so many months of joy and summer sun, but his companion, his friend, was in need and Lucius owed him a debt.

Whenever that selfish part of Lucius told him he need not go, he remembered that night in Caledonia when Einion and his sister Briana had saved him from assassins' blades in the middle of the fort of Bertha, in the heart of the Dragon's Lair. He would not have seen his family again were it not for the twin brother and sister whom the Gods had sent to aid him.

When word had come to Einion of the desolation being wrought in his ancestral lands by his tyrant uncle, Lucius had known exactly what he had to do, though he did not relish the thought. He reminded himself that he was not the only one leaving behind a loved one, for Dagon, he knew, longed to remain with Briana who had agreed to stay behind to help watch Lucius' family instead of helping her brother to take back their stolen kingdom.

Early that morning, before the light, Lucius had knelt in the temple of Apollo which he had built upon the hill with his own hands. In the light of the bronze brazier, incense smoke surrounding him, protecting him, he had prayed to Apollo, and to Venus and Epona to guard him on his journey into the southwestern reaches of Dumnonia. More so, he had asked them to protect Adara, Phoebus, and Calliope while he was away.

For some reason, he had been filled with dread of late. This surprised him. Especially as he had faced massive armies in the field, forces that likely made Caradoc of Dumnonia's army look like green recruits.

His prayers finished, he took the sword his wife had given him from the altar, and made to hang it upon the wall, a piece of him for his family to gaze upon and be comforted.

"You mustn't leave it," Adara said behind him, cloaked and silent in the shadows by the temple door as she waited for him to finish.

"But it will give you and the children comfort to know that I will be back to take it," he answered.

"It will give us more comfort to know that you have it in your hand," Adara said, walking toward him. She reached up and touched his cheek, no tears upon her face this time, for she had cried too often at his leaving. "If you have it, I will be more certain of your safe return." She picked up the sword and slid it into the scabbard at his back so that the golden, dragon-hilted blade jutted brightly behind his shoulders. "Promise me you'll return," she said, their arms about each other, her chin buried in the neckline of his thick black cloak.

They held each other firmly, ever-reluctant in their goodbyes.

"I'll be fine, my love," Lucius whispered. "I owe this to Einion and Briana."

"I know. And we'll be safe with Briana, Barta and the others here. Just look after yourself. Come back to me, my dragon."

"I will." Lucius looked at the doorway and the growing light outside. "I should go. They're waiting, and we have a long road."

Adara nodded. "You kissed the children?"

"Yes. Make sure they practice their riding and sword skills. The Dragon's children should be able to fight."

"The whole of his family can," she said, putting her hand upon the black cuirass with the winged dragon upon his chest. "Go now. And come back."

He kissed her, their eyes closed, and then a moment later, he was out the door, striding toward the southwest gate where Dagon held his horse for him.

Lucius Metellus Anguis took one last look at the fortress, even as clouds glided past the face of the rising sun. He adjusted his legs between the four saddle horns, felt the sword at his back, and turned to his companions.

"You don't have to come with me, you know," Einion said, tying back his long hair with a leather thong, and wrapping his cloak about himself as his white pony shifted nervously beneath him.

"I know. But I want to," Lucius said. "I told you I would help you get back your kingdom, and I meant it."

"As I meant it when I said you didn't have to," Einion replied.

"Are we going to sit here and argue?" Dagon said from atop his big black gelding, "or are we going to get this journey underway?"

Lucius smiled, knowing Dagon had not wanted to leave Briana's bed. It helped that this was for her benefit as well, but Dagon was ever loyal to Lucius and knew the size of the debt that Lucius owed to Einion.

Lucius stared up at the high ramparts and saw the figure of his wife standing there, her cloak whipping about her as she watched them depart.

I'll be back, my love... I'll see you soon. With that last thought, that final look, he turned Lunaris to face down the road. The stallion jumped forward and the other two followed, their hooves clicking loudly as they headed for the smoke of Lindinis in the distance.

The journey went quickly the first day as they passed Lindinis and headed toward Isca. There had been a brief delay in the small, roadside town when some of the local ordo members and merchants had recognized Lucius from their dealings with him since he had arrived with his retinue to occupy the hillfort to the northeast of the town. Their pressure upon him to get the emperor to raise the town to the status of official 'civitas' was incessant to say the least.

He did not like some of the men of Lindinis, and he was eager to get away. However, he spent some time greeting them, so near was the place to the fortress that they could indeed make his life difficult.

Lucius was acutely aware that on this journey, he was not travelling under imperial protection or orders. No imperial pass sat tucked safely in the depths of his saddle bags, no imperial seal to guarantee his safe passage. To most, he was just another armed Roman out of uniform. The red cloak of command was back in their home, and he now wore the black cloak of an assassin for all intents and purposes. The dragon armour was well-hidden beneath his thick cloak as they rode, but there was no way he would have left without it.

Dagon likewise had left his heavy, full-body scale armour and opted for a brown leather cuirass and cloak. Einion, the man whose throne they were going to take back, wore his usual leather tunic and breeches, and a long, deep-green cloak. His father's ancestral sword stood out from his hip, iron-grey and angry, awaiting the blood to come.

As they rode, Lucius and Dagon each glanced at the Briton, wondering what could be going through his head after so many years of vengeful thoughts.

They knew that Caradoc, Einion's uncle, was a man of blood and savagery. They had heard the story of how he had slain Einion and Briana's entire family, his own family. Even for men of war like Lucius and Dagon, the tale had been utterly gruesome.

II

MEMORIAE SANGUINIS

'Memories of Blood'

As the three horsemen broke free of Lindinis, they found themselves sharing the road with a greater number of merchants and drovers heading to the larger markets of Isca to the southwest. Many of the travellers stared at Lucius, Einion and Dagon as they passed, and so they rode at a quicker pace, able to break away and make better time.

They passed one night at a roadside tavern, and then continued on their way.

Lucius and Dagon tried not to interrupt Einion's thoughts overmuch as they travelled, for he was determinedly silent.

What they did not know was that he had been nursing his anger, his thirst for vengeance ever since Etain, the priestess of Ynis Wytrin, had told him now was the time to reclaim his family's lands.

Etain was, he knew, extremely powerful and aware of all that went on in Britannia, and her visions, her advice, were corroborated by scattered reports of a pestilence in the southwest, in Dumnonia.

Einion thought of the morning the priestess had called for him, to tell him the news.

"Your kingdom is dying and soon it will be no more unless you overthrow your traitor uncle."

Her words had been plain, and terrible, but Einion had been grateful as he listened to Etain's words.

"But how?" Einion asked.

"You are friend to dragons now," she said, smiling at him. "And the Gods are ready to test you. Are you ready?"

He nodded.

When he had gone to think about it, to prepare himself, Briana had stayed behind to speak further with Etain, the Druid Weylyn, and the Christian priest, Father Gilmore.

"They all agree that if this pestilence is not stopped, if our uncle is not unseated from our family lands, then even Ynis Wytrin will be in danger," Briana said from the doorway of the small home where she and her brother had taken refuge in the sacred isle for years after the massacre of their family. She nodded. "Even the children who dwell here won't be safe."

"Then I must go," he said.

Einion remembered it like it was yesterday, the firelight, the pounding of his heart as he sharpened his father's sword. It was over a week ago since that day, but the words echoed in his mind like a recurring dream. *There is a pestilence in Dumnonia...the land is dying...*

Each night as they lay down to sleep on the road, and every moment in the saddle beside Lucius and Dagon, Einion thought of that night long ago, when his family had been all but wiped out in one single slaughter, leaving only him and Briana to escape, having killed as many of their uncle's men as they could before taking their horses and riding for the moors.

The face of Caradoc, their mother's brother, floated in Einion's consciousness like a circling vulture ready for another meal. He could see the blood of his mother and father dripping like grisly honey down Caradoc's face, the blood of his siblings on the blade of his long sword...his smile as he watched Einion and Briana hack at his men.

The last Einion had seen of the formidable Caradoc was of him sitting upon his father's throne, his feet upon the savaged bodies of their parents as he took his ease.

My parents had no burial... he thought sadly. *Their souls will beg and be torn by hounds at the gates of Annwn.*

He tried to remember their home, the expanses of green and brown, windswept and soaking, the crash of waves at the bottom of the cliffs, and the call of sea birds above the fortress walls.

But his reverie was constantly broken by the cries of his family and their servants, the crash of ceramic and slither of swords as he remembered that night.

He, Briana, and Gwendolyn had been at a fire on the far side of the fortress rock, talking of the future, of their land and what Rome would do once it came deeper into Dumnonia. They had been idealistic and excited at the prospects, for the Pax Romana had settled nicely in the south, and once more, men, women and children could go about safely, more so than they had been able to in generations.

Gwendolyn had been curled in his strong arms then, her eyes alight with the flames, her hands tracing the lines of his calloused palms.

Gwendolyn... Einion gripped his reins in white knuckles as he remembered her. She had meant more to him than anyone, save Briana, and he knew that of all lost in the massacre, he missed her the most.

When the slaughter began, it was as if a Banshee had come into their midst. Screams rang out, and the clash of weapons was immediate and shocking.

Their heads whipped around as they each grabbed their weapons, always to hand, and they ran toward the low slate buildings where shadows jumped and screamed in the flickering firelight of small windows.

"Run and hide, both of you!" Einion had said to them.

"Not likely!" Briana answered, her sword slithering free.

"I'm coming with you!" Gwendolyn answered, pulling her dagger free of her belt, her long, deep green tunic up around her knees as she ran with them.

Villagers were running from the hall, screaming into the night as men in black hacked at their backs, uncaring of sex or age.

"My Prince! Help me!" one woman yelled as she scrambled toward Einion, her eyes wild with terror. Einion leapt forward to her, his sword slashing over her head at her pursuer who flew face forward into the woman he had been seeking to kill.

"Get her up!" Einion said. "Get her out of here!" he yelled at Gwendolyn, but the woman carried on running without help, careening dangerously fast toward the cliffs. "Stop her!"

Gwendolyn ran after the woman, disappearing into the night like a swooping owl. There was a scream then, and the sound of struggle.

"Gwendolyn!" Einion yelled, veering from the hall to pursue but stopping abruptly when Briana screamed her battle cry.

The sound of clanging swords drew him back to his sister's side, and together they hacked at the six men who poured from the side door of the hall.

"Leave her! Or by the Gods I'll kill you!"

They heard their father's voice from within the hall and ran for the door.

"No!!!!" the voice yelled again, followed by clanging steel. "Fiend of -"

Just as Einion and Briana cut their way into their father's hall, they saw him upon his knees, their uncle Caradoc towering over him, surrounded by his men, their father holding his guts in his arms as he stared down upon his slain wife, his eyes wide in shock.

Cunnomore of Dumnonia collapsed upon his wife, and the stench of blood and offal filled Einion and Briana's nostrils as they stared in horror at their uncle, Caradoc, who sat upon the stone, fur-covered throne and put his feet upon his slain sister and brother-in-law.

"Bastard!" Einion screamed, his sword slashing through many of the men before them as he tripped over the bodies of his father's people to get at Caradoc.

"Here he is!" Caradoc laughed, pointing at Einion and commanding his men to press in on them.

Briana reached Einion's side, her own blade taking many lives, but the press of enemies too thick to approach Caradoc.

Einion tripped at one point and fell forward upon his hands, the blood sticky upon the cobbled flooring. There, in the writhing mass of death, he spotted the hilt of his father's longsword where he had dropped it. Einion groped for it, rose up, pulled by Briana, and slashed in a huge arc to take the heads from three of his enemies.

Briana pulled at him again and together they retreated toward the side door, over bodies and out into the night, pursued by Caradoc's men like rabid wolves after a stag.

As Einion went out the door, he caught a glimpse of his uncle laughing at the sport, leaning back in his father's throne.

It was only because they knew the hidden ways of the fortress rock that Einion and Briana were able to escape that night, leading Caradoc's men to their deaths at the edges of the cliffs.

However, even with the orange-red glow of the Samhain bonfires about the rock, they almost fell from the cliffs to their deaths. They scrambled and fought their way to the rope bridge that led to the mainland where they made their way to the stables to get horses and flee for the moors.

Several of Caradoc's men, and some of the traitorous villagers rode hard after them, but the young prince and his sister had been too swift, riding at suicidal pace over the streams and along hedgerows until the dark cloaked them completely from killing eyes.

Every time Einion sat on a horse now, he remembered that night, the ride to freedom, and the loss he had left behind in the hall of his father, and upon the windswept fortress rock.

The night before they reached Isca, the three men stopped at an inn beside a wood along the Fosse Way. They were tired from the road, but grateful for the fact that the rain that usually hampered this part of Britannia had held back. Clouds loomed in the skies like sleeping wraiths, but they never opened up.

The mansio, a place called The Chariot Wheel, was well-equipped, and busy. The u-shaped structure was surrounded by a wall at the back where it faced onto a forest. There were outbuildings for the horses, and rooms on the upper level overlooking the courtyard. Most important of all was the smell of fresh bread and roasting meat that permeated the place.

"From what you've told us of the landscape in Dumnonia, Einion, I think we had better enjoy sleeping with a roof over our heads before we head into the wilds of your country." Lucius led the way off of the road and into the courtyard to a series of hitching stones on the far side of a row of wagons. "I'm paying," Lucius added as he slid from the saddle. He stretched his back and arms, and pat Lunaris.

"If that smell is anything to go by, you'll hear no arguments from me," Dagon added.

"Sounds fine," Einion said, throwing his leg over his horse's neck and sliding down. "Though you might hear me complaining of your snoring, Dagon."

"I do not!" the Sarmatian protested, turning to Lucius. "Do I?"

Lucius simply nodded, trying not to laugh.

"Briana hasn't said anything to me," Dagon mused.

"Cause she loves you, big man!" Lucius slapped him on the back and tossed a bronze as to the boy who was waiting to take care of the horses.

The three men hoisted their weapons and saddle bags, and walked toward the double front doors of the stout limestone building.

The taverna was full but for a table in a corner at the back. The clientele was mostly made up of merchants headed for Isca's markets to sell their wares, or retired veterans who had made their homes in the vicus outside Isca's walls. No matter who they were, a silence fell upon the room when Lucius stepped in, followed by his friends.

"Salve!" he said, looking to the tavern keeper at the far end. "Any room for three servants of Rome?"

21

He was not sure why he said it like that, but the feeling he had got upon entering the room urged him to play it safe after a quick scan of the faces looking in their direction.

"Come and sit!" the tavern keeper said, pointing to the vacant table. "A group just left. It's yours if you're willing to wait."

Lucius approached the bar and smiled. "No rush with smells like that coming from your kitchens. We'll take it, and food and drink for three, whatever it is you have."

Lucius removed his cloak, the heat of the place quite intense toward the back, and the inn keeper's eyes focused on the dragon upon his armoured breast.

"You lads off duty then?" he said, looking past Lucius at Dagon and Einion, his eyes resting on the latter.

"Yes," Lucius answered. "Three friends travelling to Isca."

"Hmm. I see." The man motioned to the table once more and Dagon and Einion went to sit, dropping their bags on the floor along the wall.

"Thank you," Lucius said before joining them.

"Friendly place," Dagon murmured, glancing around the room to see several men staring their way, going back to their conversations when he stared back. "All Romans here?"

"Not really," Lucius said. "Seems to be mostly retired auxiliaries and some merchants."

"No one will bother us," Einion said. *Our fight is yet to come...*

After a few minutes, a burly veteran came over to their table carrying a tray with a large clay wine jug and matching cups. He set it down on the table and stood there looking at Lucius.

"From me and the lads," the big man said, pointing to a group of veterans at the far side of the tavern.

"I'm sorry?" Lucius answered, standing. "Do I know you, soldier?"

"No, Praefectus. But we've all heard about you and what you've been doing." He nodded at the dragon on Lucius'

22

armour. "We all fought the Selgovae and Caledonii when the wall was breached thirty-odd years ago, and we know how vicious the bastards can be."

"They are that," Lucius answered, smiling. "But really, there's no need to -"

"Think nothing of it, Praefectus. Now we can say we've bought drinks for the Dragon. Something from a few humble men of the legions."

"I thank you…"

"Cassius."

"Cassius. Maybe later we can trade some battle stories?" Lucius said.

The man laughed loudly and nodded, becoming quite animated all of a sudden. "Now you're talking, lad!"

Cassius made his way back to his friends and Lucius sat down again with Einion and Dagon.

"So much for keeping a low profile," Dagon murmured as he poured the wine for the three of them.

"I have a feeling it's Einion who should keep a low profile," Lucius said, looking to the Briton.

He nodded. "It would help, yes," he said.

"You going to tell us about what happened, and what we're up against?" Dagon asked.

Einion glanced around the room and nodded. "Yes, but after we eat," he said as the inn keeper approached with a laden tray and placed it on the table in their midst.

The roast boar was delicious, and after some days on the road, surviving on dry rations, Lucius thought that he had never had anything so good. The steaming meat went down perfectly with the wine, fresh bread, and a plate of wild greens that dripped with juice from the roast.

They ate in silence for some time, watching more and more men leave the tavern to go to their rooms on the upper floor.

When they had finished, the inn keeper sent a boy to carry the men's things to their room, but the three of them kept their weapons to hand.

"Don't worry," Lucius said to the inn keeper. "Habit. They never leave our sides."

The man nodded and went away.

Cassius and his group were getting stuck into drinking, and cast an occasional glance in Lucius' direction.

Lucius however, smiled, and then turned to sit with Einion and Dagon beside a burning brazier. "All right," he said, leaning in to speak with the other two men. "Tell us."

Einion emptied his cup and, with his elbows on his knees, his long hair hanging down a little, began his tale.

He spoke for some time of that night at Samhain, about his father's fortress by the sea, and of the uncle who had betrayed them all, including his own sister, Einion and Briana's mother.

Lucius was no stranger to family betrayal and murder, his father having been in part responsible for the death of his own beloved sister, Alene. However, for some reason, Caradoc of Dumnonia sounded like a much more vicious foe. Where Lucius' father had been a cowardly politician, taken to beating his wife and younger children, Caradoc sounded like he would not shy from any fight.

"He is a warrior," Einion said. "And a formidable one." He gripped the hilt of his father's longsword as he spoke, running his fingers over the worn leather handle as if he were still seeing the blood running into every crevice and crack.

"Are you worried about fighting him?" Dagon asked. "Do you think he has a lot of warriors?"

Einion was silent for a few moments, then he nodded.

"Aye... I am worried. I hate to say it. And yes, he no doubt has many warriors."

"You're well-trained, my friend," Lucius added. "And you have right on your side."

The Briton said nothing.

"Lucius and I will make sure you have your chance at him," Dagon said. "If your people are anything like mine, it will be important that they see you defeat him in single combat."

Lucius expected Einion to shy from this, only because he seemed worried, but he surprised them both by nodding.

"I can't wait." He looked directly at Lucius and Dagon, his eyes fiery in the light of the brazier. "All those years healing and training in Ynis Wytrin, behind the mists, I have thought only of avenging my family's murder. When the Gods sent me and Briana north to find you, Lucius, I was angry at first. I thought that I would never return to Dumnonia."

"And yet, here we are," Lucius said. "And you are not alone."

"No. And I know what you both risk in coming with me. But after everything that has happened, it is meant to be like this. The Gods have something in mind. What, I don't know, but either way, there will be an end of it."

Silence fell over their circle once more.

Lucius thought of home, of Adara and the children sleeping in the warmth of their wooden hall atop the hillfort. *Now is not the time for regret or weakness,* he thought. *It's time for hardened resolve to help a friend in need.*

He noticed Cassius and the others looking his way again, and turned to Dagon and Einion.

"You can go up and get some rest. I'll spend a few minutes with the veterans over there." Lucius stood, took up his black cloak and sword, and walked over to join the retired legionaries.

"The troops seem to love him wherever he goes in this land," Einion smiled. "I guess I'm lucky to count the Dragon as my friend," he laughed.

"Yes," Dagon answered. "We both are. But Lucius needs to be careful. A well-loved commander can be seen as a danger in some circles."

25

III

IN VASTITATEM

'Into the Wild'

"In all my years of fighting, I've never seen anything like what we did north of the big wall. Fucking unbelievable savagery!"

Lucius sat back and listened politely to the reminiscences of Cassius and his friends as more wine was brought, and more logs thrown onto the brazier's flames. He was tired, and trying not to get drunk, but they were a good bunch of men, and they did not treat him like a child, as veterans had done in the early days of his career.

"Tell us, Praefectus," one leather-faced man said, leaning in. "How does fighting the tribes in Caledonia compare with where else you've been?"

"Yes, where have you been, Praefectus?" asked another.

Lucius set his cup down and crossed his arms as he stared into the flames nearby. Whenever people asked him about the battles he had fought, a part of him wanted to put them off, for the memories were too gruesome and at odds with the man he believed he was. Nobody ever asked about his family, or the wondrous things he had seen in travelling the empire. They wanted to know of battle and bloodshed.

He sighed. He could not blame the veterans, for war was all most of them had ever known.

"It's difficult to compare," Lucius began. "I've never seen anything so terrifying as a Parthian cavalry charge when I was in the infantry. It shook the earth and you couldn't see the bastards coming for all the dust they kicked up." Even then, Lucius could hear those faraway screams, the sounds of his brothers being trampled under iron-shod hooves in the desert.

"Then again, the Caledonii don't seem to have any fear. It's hard to develop a proper strategy against an enemy without fear, don't you think?"

"Aye," they each said.

"We just had to hammer at them again and again," Cassius said.

"And they still came back, right?" Lucius said.

"True enough."

"And so they may again."

"So, are you saying this new treaty won't hold, Praefectus?" one of the others ventured.

"I'm not saying that exactly." Lucius knew he needed to be careful about what he said. "You all know the Caledonii. How long has Rome been trying to subdue that country?"

"A long time," Cassius agreed.

A vision of an ancient tree with the bodies of his men dangling from its limbs came into Lucius' mind, and he shivered beneath his armour. Nodding, he said, "Give me a charge of Parthian cavalry any day."

"Really?" they asked.

"At least they fight you in the open," Lucius added.

The men thought about that and nodded, though some seemed unconvinced.

Lucius did not care. If he was truthful, he was getting tired of all the fighting.

"So where to next for you, Praefectus? You and your friends are heading to Isca you said?"

"That's right, Cassius. Thought we'd check it out. I also have some business I need to take care of."

"Hmm." Cassius looked oddly at Lucius as he rose.

"I thank you all for your hospitality. It's been good getting to know you."

"To the Dragon!" a few of the men slurred, raising cups and splashing their wine.

Lucius laughed and mock-bowed, but his face grew dark as he stepped away.

Cassius followed after him.

"Praefectus, wait!"

"Yes?" Lucius stopped in a spot of moonlight that was angling in through one of the windows.

"I don't mean to pry, but you and your friends don't seem to be heading into town for pleasure." Cassius put up his hands. "Don't get me wrong. I don't expect you to tell me nothing. A man's business is his own. I just want to say that things is different in Isca than elsewhere. It's full of politicians - you know the sort. Anyway, if you're in need of anything, in town or out of it, you can count on my friend Flaccus. He's centurion at the western gate of the city. Big tall bastard, red hair. You can't miss him. You tell him you're a friend of mine and he'll do what he can for you, whatever it is."

"I thank you, Cassius," Lucius said. "But really, we're just out for a bit of fun."

"Like I said, a man's business is his own. But brothers-in-arms need to look after each other, right?"

"Right." Lucius smiled and grasped the man's arm. "Thank you again."

"Praefectus," Cassius said, saluting and going back to his friends, some of whom were already asleep in their chairs by the fire.

Lucius turned towards the moonlight that was shining in at the window and felt its coolness upon his skin. The moon was close to full. It was soothing. The rain had stopped, and the world outside was serene and inviting.

He put his cloak on and, grasping his sword in his left hand, went out the door. The air was chilly, and he pulled his hood up. Apart from two stable boys playing knucklebones by a small lamp at the entrance to the stables, no one was around. Lucius looked up and saw thin black wisps of cloud gliding silently overhead, dancing in the face of the silvery light. Nightingales sang in the forest around the back of the mansio, and Lucius followed the sound, his boots squelching in the damp grass as he rounded the corner of the building and approached a gap in the surrounding wall where it led onto an open field.

He turned to face the moon where it hovered above the inn's rooftop, and closed his eyes for a moment. He slowed his breathing and imagined he was invisible to the rest of the world. He could hear his heartbeat in his ears, and when he opened his eyes to see the moon again, the field was filled with mist that surrounded him like lake water up to the knees.

"Far-shooting Apollo... The farther I go from my family, the more wary I become of the task ahead of us. I know Briana and Barta are with Adara and the children, but please watch over them while I am away." Lucius walked a bit farther into the field, the dark forest looming at the edge where the stubble of the recently harvested crop was hidden beneath the mist.

"Guide me on this journey, oh Far-Shooter. Guide me as you always have."

On the rooftop then, the silhouette of a crow appeared before the moon, and Lucius turned to see it, surprised by the harsh sound it made.

"My Lord?" Lucius whispered.

I am here, Metellus.

Lucius whipped around to see Apollo standing before him a few feet away, his light dissolving the mist that surrounded them and giving everything an icy glow.

Lucius fell to one knee, his head bowed beneath the hood of his cloak.

Stand, Metellus. After so many years, are you still surprised that I come when you call? Is your faith so shaken?

"No, my Lord. Not at all." Lucius calmed himself with a few deep breaths, and then rose to his feet, his head still bowed. He struggled to calm his shaking limbs, for it was always thus in the presence of the Gods.

Be at ease, Apollo said, his thick arm rising from the folds of his blue cloak to touch Lucius' forehead. *The Dragon needs his rest.*

Lucius looked up at the eyes staring at him, those fearful orbs where the heavens whirled and time had no meaning.

"Will you watch over my family when I am gone, as you have always done?" Lucius asked.

Your family is safe under the protection of your friends, do not fear for them.

"Thank you -"

It is for your sake that I come now. Apollo's gaze was stern then, but it also held something more.

Lucius tried to place it, but he could not gaze too long at the immortal before him.

I have come to warn you against this quest, Apollo said.

Lucius pushed back his hood and looked up again. "Warn me?" he said. "But I must help my friend, Lord. I owe him a life-debt."

You do not need to go.

"But I would help him," Lucius insisted, shrinking a little as he did so.

You are ever-stubborn, Apollo said, walking past Lucius to gaze up at the stars in the heavens he knew so well. *I've watched over you since the day you came into this world, Lucius Metellus Anguis.* The god's voice hinted at nostalgia and pride, but there was also fear there. *I've seen you through many trials... I've seen you fall, and get back up again. I've allowed you to fend for yourself when it was needed, and come to your aid when other forces were against you...*

"And I am ever grateful to you, my Lord. Have I been lacking in some way? Have my prayers and offerings not reached you?" Lucius worried now, for he had never heard his protector speak thus.

They have, Apollo assured him, *but you must know that in the days to come, as you head into the wild lands belonging to your friend, I will not be able to help you.*

Lucius stopped at this, and wondered if he had ever taken the Gods' protection for granted. He had felt invincible on the field of battle since his early days, though he had known great fear. But now, the thought of his god's protection being withheld, for whatever reason, was something he could not grasp. He thought he must have done something.

"My Lord, if I have offended you, Venus, or Epona in any way, I am truly sorry. I have always done my best to earn the faith you have shown in me."

I know. And no, you have not disappointed, for you always persevere. But the place to which you are headed, and about which I am not permitted to speak, is a realm outside of my power.

"Dumnonia?"

I cannot say, Apollo shook his head and his eyes blazed as if he were near to breaking a vow. *I urge you to turn back.*

The words were uttered in deadly earnest, and they struck Lucius to the bone with fear. He thought of all the sacrifices that others had made for him, of the gratitude he had shown them, and of how it had never felt like quite enough after the fact. True, he had saved many lives, but there were many he had not been able to wrestle from Death's dark claws - Hippogriff and his turmae in Caledonia, Coilus of the Votadini, Alerio...Alene...

Now that he had a chance to help one of his closest friends to regain his throne and avenge the deaths of almost his entire family, he felt that he could not refuse, even if a god asked him to withdraw.

"My Lord, you send fear to the depths of my heart with your words," Lucius said, staring at the ground about his feet, imagining blood filling the furrows in the soil. "But who would I be if I withdrew my aid from a man, a friend, who has saved my life on more than one occasion? It is the only thing he has ever asked of me. Can I abandon him at such a time?"

Apollo smiled sadly. He had known what Lucius' answer would be before he ever appeared to him. It had been a selfish attempt on his part to save his favourite from the possibilities that lay ahead.

31

Your courage runs deeper than your fears, young dragon, Apollo said. *You must do as your conscience instructs you, but I will tell you one thing.*

"Yes, Lord?"

Hold your wife's god-sent gift ever in your hand.

"Lord?"

I must go, Apollo said, growing in height as if to be nearer the stars above, his cloak billowing like a stormy night sky. Then his eyes focused on Lucius'. *Be strong.*

Lucius blinked at the flash of silver light, and when he looked once again, Apollo was gone, and he was surrounded by the early morning mist.

He thought about pleading to the darkness, apologizing for his disregard of Apollo's warning, but he knew it was too late. He also knew he had made up his mind, despite the seed of fear in the pit of his gut.

After a few deep breaths, he began to walk back toward the shadow of the mansio, noticing that the crow no longer stood upon the rooftop. He wondered if he would ever see it again.

The three of them were on the road to Isca early, after breaking their fast on honey and steaming bread fresh from the oven behind the mansio.

Lucius had not slept, his mind going over Apollo's warnings. He was determined not to tell Dagon or Einion about what had happened, though they were well aware of his occasional contact with the Gods. Some things were better left unsaid.

Dagon was cheerful after a good night's sleep, but Einion remained brooding.

It's no wonder, Lucius thought, *with all the pressure of the task ahead.*

All three of them wondered what they would find once they entered Einion's kingdom.

"What did your veteran friends have to say last night?" Dagon asked as they rode at a trot down the last stretch of sunlit road before Isca. "Anything useful?"

"Just trading war stories," Lucius said. "They've all had their encounters with the Caledonii."

Dagon's face grew dark. "If we ever have to fight them again, I won't rest until every last one lies dead upon the field and our walls are covered with their bleeding heads."

"Easy, my friend," Lucius urged. "That fight is for another day. Focus on what lies directly ahead."

"We'll need to stop in Isca for some supplies," Einion said suddenly.

"My thoughts exactly," Lucius added.

"There's little food upon the moors, and at this time, the harvests will have been brought in for the new year."

"I thought the new year was in Januarius?" Dagon said.

"Not in Dumnonia. The festival of Samhain at the end of this month is the death of the old year."

Dagon shifted uncomfortably in his saddle.

"Then may Janus lead you to a new beginning, my friend," Lucius said to Einion. "One thing Cassius did say is that if we needed anything at all, we should go to his friend Flaccus, a centurion at the west gate. Apparently the man is trustworthy."

"Risky without an imperial pass, Lucius, though a little help is better than none," Dagon said.

"Hopefully we won't need him," Einion said. "I just want to get the supplies and move on into Dumnonia as quick as we can."

Einion dug his heels into his mount's flanks and the horse sped off down the road.

"You heard the man," Dagon said, smiling as he yipped and sped after the Briton.

In the early days of the Roman invasion of Britannia, Isca had been the site of a castrum for the II Augustan legion. It was a big site, all of ninety-two acres with high walls and the

33

standard grid pattern of any Roman fortification. It guarded the water that led to the sea on the south side.

Isca Dumnoniorum, as it was known, was the administrative capital of Dumnonia at the end of the Fosse Way, one of Britannia's major routes. After the legion had finished with Isca, and moved on to a new base at Caerleon, the city had become the official civitas of Dumnonia.

As they came closer to the broad earthen ditches topped with aged stone walls, Lucius noticed that troops dotted the ramparts, more than was usual in a peaceful civitas. The enclosed town slept like a behemoth beside the river, voices and smoke rising from within the walls. A steady stream of people from the vici on two sides flowed into the northern gate.

"Looks like we'll need to walk through the town," Lucius said as he reined in and they dismounted.

Carts rolled past them in the direction of the gate where troopers questioned people and checked their cargoes.

Lucius, Einion and Dagon waited their turn, their eyes scanning the crowds.

Behind them, a large group that had been travelling in the same direction now joined the line.

It had been some time since Lucius had been in such a busy place, and he felt himself tensing up in the press of flesh, leather and damp wool.

The livestock yards to the southeast of the town resonated with the lowing of cattle and the squeal of pigs.

"People come from all around to sell their wares and their livestock here in Isca," Einion said as they stepped closer. "We also traded here."

"What did your family sell?" Dagon asked.

"Moor ponies from our herds. They were the best around."

"Any old acquaintances we should be worrying about, who might recognize you?" Lucius asked.

"I don't know. I didn't come often. My father's steward came in his stead." Einion was silent a moment. "He's probably dead now." *Like Gwendolyn.*

They stepped up to the trooper at the gate, Lucius going first.

"What's your purpose in Isca?" the optio asked without looking at Lucius, continuing to write on one of the many wax tablets hanging from his cingulum.

"My friends and I are going hunting on the moors and we need some supplies."

"What, in the name of Mars, would you want to do that for?" the man said, looking up to see the dragon on Lucius' cuirass and then looking at his two armed companions. "Who are you?"

"We're off-duty soldiers from near Lindinis. Just out for a bit of sport. We won't be here longer than a couple of hours."

"Do I know you?" the man said, looking at Lucius again.

"Don't think so," Lucius answered. "But we're all brothers-in-arms, aren't we?"

"Aye, true enough." The man relaxed, ignoring the haranguing from the folks farther down the line, unhappy with the delay. "What outfit you with? You look like auxiliaries."

"We've been fighting in the North with the Cohors III Britannorum."

The man stared at the cuirass again and took an involuntary step backward. "I've heard about you," he said.

"Just another soldier fighting for the empire," Lucius said getting a little nervous now as people were leaning in to listen. "Can we pass?"

"Yes, uhh, Praefectus. Of course. If you've a mind, the baths are newly refurbished by the collegia. Feel free to stay and enjoy them. They're worth it."

"My thanks, soldier," Lucius said, nodding politely and moving past the man with Einion and Dagon behind him.

They passed beneath the big stone gatehouse and came out the other side onto a busy thoroughfare, the eyes of the legionaries atop the walls watching as they led their horses into the crowd.

Lucius spotted the rooftop of the basilica and the smoke from the baths. "The forum will be there. We can get our supplies, and then be on our way."

"No baths?" Dagon joked.

"No," Lucius chuckled.

"Besides," Einion added. "If you're worried about getting clean, we'll come to the rains soon enough."

They continued walking, but after a few steps, Lucius stopped and looked back. He had felt as though someone had been watching him very intently, but in that crowd, there was no way to know.

"Watch your denarii, my friends," he said. "The cut-purses are out."

It was slow going through the streets, especially since they were leading their horses and trying to keep on eye on their saddlebags at the same time. For the most part, folk steered clear of the three warriors, but they were watched with wary eyes from a distance.

Isca was smaller than other Roman towns like Londinium and Eburacum, but it had all the amenities of a proper civitas. The buildings lining the streets were low, one and two-storey structures, most with terracotta roof tiles. Some of the private dwellings and merchant offices facing onto the street were more ornate, painted in gaudy colours, their roofs decorated with acanthus and gorgon head finials.

They passed a theatre on their right and then the street seemed to bottle-neck, slowing their progress even more. However, the rising voices and sweet tang of smoke led Lucius to believe they were close to the forum and market, and soon enough, the crowd spilled into the large open square before the basilica, like an arena crowd flowing out of the Colosseum's vomitoria.

They scanned the edges of the forum and the awnings that indicated the food sellers, for they needed no weapons or wool, armed as they were for war and not a gentle country stroll.

Einion remained with the horses, keeping a low profile while Lucius and Dagon pushed their way to the front of the crowds to get some dried meat, cheese wrapped in cloth, bread, oat cakes, and a small amphora of wine from Hispania.

"You're carrying that," Dagon said to Lucius.

Lucius laughed. "You don't want any?"

"Of course I do!"

"Good. Then you can help carry it." Lucius punched him playfully and moved on to join Einion who was looking anxious to get going. "Anything wrong?" Lucius asked him.

Einion, his cloak hood up, indicated the fountain in the middle of the forum. "See those three men in matching brown tunics and cloaks?"

"Yeah," Dagon said, peering over Einion's shoulder. "The ones that look like Praetorians?"

Lucius gripped the pommel of his sword where it hung concealed beneath his cloak.

"Don't you think they're a long way from base?" Einion said.

Lucius nodded, continuing to put the food in the empty saddle bags on Lunaris' back. "I saw them at the gate when we came in too. They were on the road with the other travellers behind us."

"This could ruin everything," Einion said.

"Should we split up?" Dagon asked, fingering the handle of his own sword.

"No," Lucius said, handing Dagon the small amphora of wine to strap to his mount. "We stay together and avoid any fight." He took Lunaris' reins from Einion and, for a moment, thought about going over to confront the men. But he thought better of it. He was not on army or imperial business, and so he had much less protection than in the past. As far as others were concerned, he was a civilian on this journey.

Even Apollo told me he cannot protect me... he thought with regret.

"Einion, do we need anything else you can think of here?" Lucius asked.

"No. We should go."

"Shouldn't we go to the temple and make an offering?" Dagon added.

"The Gods will understand if we wait," Lucius said. "I've got an idea. Come."

With that, Lucius led the way through the crowd once more, out the far end of the forum, past a group of temples, and toward the western gate that led to the bridge over the river.

"Hold there!" the soldiers at the gate halted the three horsemen and surrounded them from a distance. They were much more disciplined than at the other gate, Lucius noticed.

A burly centurion walked directly toward them, the horizontal crest of his helmet high and bristling, a thick, smooth vinerod held tightly in his beefy fist.

Lucius noticed the scarred forearms and the red hair jutting out from beneath his helmet. He swept his cloak back to reveal his cuirass.

"Where do you boys think you're going?" the centurion said.

"Are you centurion Flaccus?" Lucius asked.

The man stepped closer, so close he was looking down on Lucius' head.

"Who wants to know?"

"My name is Metellus. Your friend Cassius up the road at The Chariot's Wheel told me that I could rely on you to help us out if we needed it."

"Cassius?" The man relaxed a little and stepped back, only then seeing the dragon upon Lucius' armour. "You a man of the legions then?"

"Yes."

"I don't see why -" Recognition dawned on Flaccus' face and his demeanour became much more respectful. "Are you..."

"Yes, he is," Dagon added. "And we're his guard."

Flaccus looked at both Einion and Dagon and then back at Lucius.

"What are you doing here, Praefectus? Not many go out onto the moors, especially these days."

"What do you mean? Why not?" Einion asked, stepping closer.

The troopers around them closed in at the sudden movement, but Flaccus waved them down.

"They say there's a pestilence on the moors. People been showing up with boils on their bodies, or blackened skin. Some say there's madness there. There's talk of storms, birds falling dead out of the sky, poisonous mists, and bog monsters that creep out to grab a whole horse and rider as they pass. The few we let through don't come back at all."

"How long has this been going on?" Einion could not help asking, but Flaccus did not seem to mind telling.

"Been happening for some time, but it's been said that things got worse a couple of years ago maybe."

Lucius glanced behind them and thought that he saw some forms lingering in the shadows.

"There was also..." Flaccus stopped talking when one of the other troopers shook his head, like he had known what his centurion was about to say.

"What?" Lucius asked, turning back to the big man. "You were saying?"

"Well, just stories really, but one man who came back said he was attacked by some kinda *wyrm*, as the locals say it. I thought it was a load of bollocks, but then again..." Flaccus noticed some movement down the street and paused to look.

"Did you send any troops to check it out?" Dagon asked.

"We did," Flaccus said. "The man who came back mumbling of a wyrm was one of them."

"What happened to them?" Lucius asked.

"Whole contubernium was wiped out, and the trooper who survived hanged himself two weeks later."

Einion and Lucius exchanged looks. Lucius leaned in closer to Flaccus so only he could hear.

"Centurion, I know you've been asked to restrict access, and I hear you about the dangers out there... But my friends and I need to go that way."

"Why would you want to do that? You won't be coming back, sir," Flaccus said, his thick arms flexing where they crossed over the phalerae decorating his chest harness. "What'll you do?"

"I'm not allowed to say, but it's important to the stability of Dumnonia."

"Hmph. Pardon me, Praefectus, but *stability*'s not really a word I'd use for the wilds out there."

Lucius said no more, but looked at Flaccus in earnest, waiting for the man to make up his mind. After a few moments, the centurion nodded, regret haranguing the back of his mind.

"All right. But if anyone asks, sir, we didn't see you."

"I understand, Centurion. My thanks to you men." Lucius turned to look behind them and then leaned in again. "There is problem I could use your help with."

"What's that, sir?" Flaccus said warily.

"Down the street behind us are three men who have been following us for some time. They mean to stop us."

"Why would they do that?" Flaccus asked.

"I don't know, but they are no friend of good, honest soldiers," Lucius said. "They're posing as Praetorians."

At this Flaccus looked uneasy.

"Don't worry. They aren't. But they're up to no good. If you can keep them from crossing the river, I'd be grateful."

Flaccus' face was unreadable for a minute, but then he gripped his vinerod and smiled. "We'll see what we can do," he said, winking quickly at Lucius. "You best get going then. They're coming now."

Lucius extended his hand and took Flaccus' arm. "Thank you, Centurion."

"You stay safe out there, Praefectus," he said. "If you come back out of Dumnonia in one piece, I'll know the stories I've heard about you are true. Go now." He turned to speak to the men manning the gate. "Let'em through!"

A moment later, the oak and iron doors of Isca grated open to reveal a short stretch of road running down toward the river where a stone bridge made up of several arches traversed the swift-flowing water.

Lucius, Dagon and Einion mounted up, made their way through the gates at a normal pace, and headed for the other side of the river.

They glanced back when they heard raised voices, and saw Flaccus' red cloak swinging as his vinerod swept across the face of one of their would-be followers while the troops restrained the others.

Someone's voice was cut short, and Lucius knew that at least one of them was dead. He had heard enough such cries to know when it was lethal.

"We'd better pick up the pace," he said to Dagon, noticing that Einion was already a ways ahead, racing toward his home.

Dagon followed, leaving Lucius to bring up the rear.

Lucius stayed for a moment to look at the river flowing past the high walls and red rooftops of Isca, the smoke rising from the baths, the sound of voices rising from the lively forum - it felt strange at that moment to be leaving it all behind.

Once they were across the river, once he looked at the town and then toward the open moors in the distance, he truly felt like he was leaving civilization behind.

Etain's words to Einion were front of mind then, as were the warnings of Flaccus.

Lucius touched the dragon upon his cuirass and gazed to the northeast, toward home and his family. He wanted to yell to them, to call their names, but they now felt too far out of reach.

I'll be back... he thought, willing Adara to hear him.

With that, he turned Lunaris and the stallion sped off in pursuit of the others, already farther down the road, headed into the wild.

IV

VENATOR

'The Hunter'

They rode through a constant mist of rain beneath an iron grey sky where the clouds seemed willing enough to crush them upon the earth. The Roman road, a thing from the early days after the conquest of the South, was badly broken and unkept. The land was wide and open, despite the poor visibility, and mostly covered with sharp yellow gorse and heath. Occasionally, they would pass by a few towering elms, but for the most part, what trees they did see where short and windswept, as if clawed into oddly pained shapes by the winds of that ancient land.

They pressed on, Einion seemingly familiar with the lay of the land, but constantly on the lookout for the horrible changes to his home that had been described by the Roman centurion, Flaccus.

The realms of that place changed over and over, from sparse woodland, to grassland, and heathland. On and on they rode, avoiding riding over the patches of red, green and brown bog moss that Einion pointed out would swallow a horse and rider.

Einion rode ahead, and at one point, the Briton stood upon a distant boulder that seemed to swell out of the ground like the head of a giant. He gazed out into the haze of deep green and brown, his eyes scanning the land.

Lucius and Dagon eventually caught up with him, and that was only because darkness had begun to descend.

"Einion! We need to talk!" Lucius was trying not to get angry, for he suspected how Einion must feel, coming back to this land after so long, but they needed to talk, to strategize, to stay together. They all knew people got lost on the moors, and with the weather against them, it would be easy to ride off a ridge or have one of the horses snap a leg on the rough terrain.

"What's going through his mind, I wonder?" Dagon said, looking at Einion's cloaked figure ahead of them.

"What would you be thinking of, were you him?" Lucius said.

"Of killing the man who slew my family."

Lucius handed Dagon Lunaris' reins and walked over to join Einion on the boulder.

The road sloped away from their vantage point to what seemed to be the ruins of a Roman fort.

"Is that one of ours?" Lucius asked.

"One of Rome's, yes," Einion said, as he took a deep breath. "I haven't seen one person the entire time we've been riding, Lucius. Do you think they're all dead? Every person in my father's kingdom?"

"I don't know, my friend. But we need to go slowly from here on so we aren't taken by surprise. Come." Lucius put his hand on Einion's shoulder and together they returned to Dagon and the horses, the wet ground squelching beneath their boots.

"We need to talk about what Flaccus told us," Lucius said. "Has there ever been disease and madness here before?"

"I don't recall any," Einion said, worry etched on his face. "I've heard of people going mad after getting lost on the moors, or disappearing if they wandered inadvertently onto the bogs, but nothing more. Nothing like a pestilence."

"What about this wyrm thing, Flaccus mentioned?" Dagon said as he scanned the terrain.

Einion turned away from them for a moment, but did not speak right away. He shook his head, the water dripping from his long hair as he did so.

"There were stories when I was young…"

"About what?" Lucius asked.

"About…but it can't be!" Einion shook his head. "I thought it was to frighten children from wandering away from the villages and onto the moors."

"What stories?" Dagon said.

"My father told us once that in the deepest parts of the moors, when the moon was high and full, and the great hunt was ready to set out, that there was a dragon that emerged from an ancient lair. A terrible beast that could devour entire flocks of sheep and whole cattle, but that could not be sated unless but by human flesh."

"Are you serious?" Dagon said, his face grave. "You sure this wasn't just a story?"

"I used to think so, but not now," Einion said. "I haven't been to my homeland in so long..."

Lucius rubbed his face and closed his eyes against the driving rain for a moment. Something told him this was not a child's story, but that it was real and that they were about to face something more terrible than any Caledonian ambush.

A dragon? Lucius thought, his fingers going to the image upon his breast.

Einion looked at the other two and nodded unconvincingly. "It must be a story."

They were all silent for a moment. There was a ripple of thunder across the sky.

"We should take shelter for the night," Dagon said. "The fort ruins seem like as good a place as any." He pointed to the overgrown earthworks of the ramparts and the broken walls spreading out from the collapsed gatehouse.

Einion did not speak at this, but Lucius noticed his eyes searching the distant shadows.

"I agree," Lucius said. "We should dig in and get a fire going."

Normally, for Lucius, the inside of a Roman fort was a place of security and comfort, but not in that place.

As they passed through the broken gatehouse, their boots and horses' hooves treading on splintered wood, scattered iron nails, and broken masonry, they searched for any signs of recent activity, but none could be seen. The fort seemed to have been abandoned for some time, though normally when the army left a site, they dismantled it so that enemies could not make use of it. Not so in this lonely outpost upon the moors of Dumnonia.

They led the horses down the muddy path that had once been the via Decumana, their eyes searching the shadows for any threats, but all that was there were the broken pieces of Rome's presence, vine-covered ruins, and dampness.

"This looks good!" Dagon called from one of the old barrack buildings which still had three walls that appeared to be more solid than anything else. "At least it'll block the wind."

Lucius walked down the length of the barracks and saw another part that would be suitable for the horses.

"Good enough," he said, and they began unsaddling the horses.

It was not long before a fire was burning bright and warm in the former barracks, and the three men sitting around the fire passed the wine around and chewed on some of the dried meet and bread they had purchased in Isca.

Above the broken rooftops of the fortlet, the moon was burning behind the clouds as they whipped by, a sickly yellow in the sky.

Einion had been staring at it, silent as Lucius and Dagon took stock of their supplies.

After feeding the horses some of the oats they had brought along, Lucius sat back down beside Einion.

"Is there anyone you can trust when we get there?" Lucius asked.

Dagon stopped chewing and looked at Einion.

"I told you... They were all killed. I doubt my uncle would have let anyone live."

"Surely he wouldn't want to kill everyone?" Dagon said. "He'd need people to rule over, to till the earth."

"I'm sure that any person who would have been loyal to my family and escaped the slaughter of that night would have been eliminated by Caradoc. There was never any reasoning behind his actions."

"Even a mad man has his own reasons," Lucius said. "Maybe some survived?"

Einion shook his head and stared into the fire, haunted by the wounds of that night in the Summer of his life.

Lucius put his hand out and gripped his shoulder. "Whatever awaits us, or whatever help there is or isn't, we'll help you get your throne back."

Dagon stared at the two men across the fire from him. *How lucky he is to be able to even try.* He thought of his uncle, Mar, king and lord of his people. A good man cut down by a poisoned arrow. He had been a true king, and now Dagon carried his sacred sword and the kingship of his people. *But of what kingdom am I ruler? Rome took that from our people long ago.*

Dagon had, of course, come to accept his people's fate - such was the price of losing in battle to the Romans - and he would not follow any other man besides Lucius, the Dragon. But since Dagon had agreed to help Einion and Briana reclaim their kingdom, his mind had drifted back to the lands of his childhood, the grassy plains north of the Black Sea where he could ride for days without end, where the wind howled through Sarmatia's dragon banners. He wondered what had happened to his own people, those who did not ride with him in war under the Roman banners. Did they stay behind and till the earth, or continue to rear the sacred herds of horses upon the plains? It was a dream of long-ago, of stories his uncle told, and now it was like a wound opened anew.

"This moon is playing with my mind," Dagon said, aware of the other two men looking at him.

"You all right?" Lucius asked.

"I'm fine. Burden of kingship," he muttered, then looked at Einion. "You need to have some hope that there are survivors, people loyal to you and your family. The Gods don't reward despair. For your people, whoever and however many they are, you need to be strong."

Lucius smiled, and Einion nodded.

Though Dagon was the youngest of the three of them, he seemed infinitely wiser in that moment, worthy of the sacred charge of his people, which he had been given by his kin and king before him.

Lucius took the first watch as Einion and Dagon slept with their ghosts. It was certainly a lonely place, and he could imagine the men posted there going mad after a while.

The wind picked up and raced about the surrounding heathland. It slammed into rock formations and gnarled trees, and the sounds it produced were as if an army of wraiths were at the fort's gates. Tentatively, Lucius stoked the fire, added more fuel, and picked up a torch in his left hand, his sword in his right. He then went to check on the horses.

Lunaris turned and sniffed loudly when Lucius poked his head in.

"It's ok, boy. Just doing my rounds." Lucius pat the stallion and moved on down one of the rubble-strewn streets toward the centre of the fort. The wind blew away the clouds with a sudden force, like a heavy man blowing out an eight-headed lamp. The moonlight burst down upon the fort then, lighting the streets and casting shadows all around.

Lucius held out his blade, prodding the silvery light as he went, until finally he reached what must have been the principia courtyard.

All around the edges were fallen columns and shattered roof tiles. The entire area was choked with vines and thorns that had seemingly strangled the life out of the place, or else claimed it back. At the centre of the courtyard, Lucius noticed a rectangular shape. It was about waist-high and covered in vines.

After a few swings of his sword to cut some thorny branches that curled before him, he arrived at the feature. He set the torch down and pushed away the tresses of vines that covered it, to reveal a moss-covered altar. He brushed away the soft green growth and proceeded to clear the rest. When he was done, he picked up the torch and held it up to see the inscription above the image of a helmeted god holding a spear.

To Mars, God of War
Dedicated by Decius, centurion, and his men.
May our blood soak the earth and satisfy you.

Lucius wondered if he should say a prayer and offer something to Mars and to the spirits of that place. He and the God of War had often been at odds in the past, but somehow, now, Lucius knew that he could use Mars' strength. But he could not forget Apollo's warning that he was beyond the Gods' aid if he went into Dumnonia.

A sudden scream shattered the darkness outside of the fort. Lucius whipped around, sword out. He ran in the direction of the gate and stopped suddenly on the road where it crossed the outer ditches. The torch's orange light only reached a few feet into the darkness of the moor beyond.

The scream came again, much louder this time, coming closer.

"Who's out there?" Lucius called, walking farther out.

The shape emerged like a haze out of the windy darkness, a screaming girl, barefoot, wearing a woollen tunic that looked like rough tree bark.

Then the sound of a hunting horn and baying hounds exploded some distance away, a loud, echoing and eerie sound to drive fear into any person.

"Come here!" Lucius called to the girl as she ran toward the torchlight. "Hurry! Who's chasing you?"

She kept looking behind her, the sound of the horn making her shut her eyes and shudder, her black hair stuck to the tears upon her face.

Lucius reached out to her, but she ran past him, swift as a deer, and into the fort. He thought about going after her, but the sound of the horn, hounds, and hoofbeats shook the ground around him.

"Who's there?" Lucius called out loudly, his sword and torch ready. "Show yourself!" he challenged.

The hoofbeats became louder and louder, the horn deafening, and a moment later, a black form exploded out of the shadows and into the circle of orange light about Lucius.

He could not help taking a couple steps back at the sight before him.

A rider sat atop an immense jet-black horse, staring down at Lucius with green eyes that seemed to throb angrily in the middle of his perfect, death-pale face. He appeared tall, lean, agile and violent, ready to kill at any moment.

"You spoiled my hunt," the man said in a low, even voice that sounded as if it could explode from peace to violence at any moment.

But Lucius stood his ground now and stepped forward over the ground he had given. However, red eyes hovered in the darkness beyond the rider, and the faces of three hounds emerged from behind. Then Lucius noticed them: black antlers sprouting from the rider's head of thick black hair like solid burnished trunks from charred earth.

"Who are you, and why are you hunting that girl?" Lucius demanded, his sword out.

The rider's horse spun and he dismounted with a sweep of his deep green cloak. On the ground, he was two heads taller than Lucius. All the while, his hounds, massive beasts, stood watching, pawing the ground, as if waiting for a word of attack from their master.

"Lucius!" Dagon and Einion's voices echoed from within the ruined fort.

The girl must have found them, Lucius thought.

"You have no idea what you are doing, Roman," the rider said, unsheathing a long blade that was like to a deadly palm frond, or the fang of some ancient beast.

"I know exactly what I'm doing, hunter," Lucius growled. "Now tell me why you torture that girl?"

"Fool," the rider paced back and forth now, like a caged panther in the pits of the colosseum, awaiting the games. "You have no idea with whom you speak." Then those green fire-eyes focussed on Lucius' breastplate and the rider smiled. "And yet, I know you...Dragon."

"Lucius!" Dagon and Einion burst through the gate then and arrived at Lucius' side, their swords out.

In a moment, the man was upon his horse, staring down at them. "No man can stop my hunting, and go unpunished." He looked at Lucius and shook his antlered head. "The nymph is not worth what you risk." He then stared at Einion and smirked. "And you!" he laughed. "You are late to the lands that are no longer yours. Proper payment for hiding in the shadows the whole of your life."

Lucius expected defiant words from Einion beside him, but none came. He could see Einion's sword arm shaking, though he stood defiantly beside Lucius and Dagon.

"Let me cut him down, Anguis," the latter said. "You dare threaten the Dragon?" Dagon stepped forward, his sword raised.

The rider laughed loudly then, and his horse reared, even as he put his horn to his thin red lips and blew loudly upon it.

The three men covered their ears for the painful crash of that fell horn, and when they looked again, the rider and his hounds were gone.

"Where's the girl?" Lucius asked the other two, looking around behind them and into the darkness of the fort.

"What girl?" Dagon said.

"The one he was hunting! The one who ran in there and warned you both?"

51

Dagon looked at Einion who was still staring into the darkness, and then back at Lucius. "I didn't see any girl."

"She was screaming," Lucius explained. "Was wearing a brown tunic and went running into the fort."

"Maybe she's hiding," Dagon said.

Lucius pushed past them and ran into the fort in the direction he had seen the girl go. After several minutes, he returned to Einion and Dagon outside the fort gates where they had been watching to see if the rider returned.

"Find her?" Dagon asked.

"No. Not a sign of her."

"You won't find anything, Lucius," Einion finally explained. "That was Gwyn ap Nudd, the…"

"The what?"

"The Lord of the Underworld and of the Wild Hunt."

Lucius froze then, as if a cold hand had just gripped his bare spine and squeezed.

"You sure?" Lucius asked.

"Yes. Every October, as the Romans call this month, he rides out on his hunt night after night, until the great Wild Hunt at Samhain when the dead ride across the land."

Dagon sheathed his sword and made a sign against evil.

"We've angered him," Einion said, sitting heavily on a log that lay in the road near the gates. "He will not leave us in peace."

"We've dealt with gods before," Lucius said.

"Not like him, you haven't," Einion said. "Not like him…"

Lucius slept little after that, his mind racing with images of horned shadows, and hounds with dripping fangs. He searched his consciousness for the memory of the girl, a nymph, he supposed. She had seemed real, and the rider had been truly angry - though Lucius suspected his anger could be much worse, judging from the fear he had seen in Einion's eyes.

When they woke before dawn to a misting rain that covered the moors, they prepared to set out on a westward course across the deepest parts of the moors.

"We can't see the sun," Dagon pointed out. "How can you be sure we're headed in the right direction?"

"I grew up here," Einion said, "and I've travelled this road to revenge enough times in my dreams to know the way."

Dagon thought of the strange rider they had confronted the night before, and he wondered if Einion had seen that part in his dreams.

"By the end of the day, we should reach one of the outlying villages of my family's lands."

"Do you think you will have friends there?" Dagon said

"We'll see." Einion buckled the last strap of his saddle girth and took the reins of his horse.

"I'll see you at the gates," Lucius said, taking up the small amphora of wine and Lunaris' reins. "There's something I need to do."

Lucius went down the street flanking the broken barracks and picked his way back to the altar he had seen the night before. The central square of the small fort was different in the dim daylight, the stone altar seeming to fight against the binding vines of its own accord to reach the choked light above.

Lucius let go of Lunaris' reins to let him chew on some nettle while he stepped up to the altar with the amphora held in both hands. He tilted his head up to the sky and felt the rain wetting his face lightly.

Two crows perched themselves on the broken battlements, staring down at him, their bodies black against the white sky.

Lucius looked down at the altar and then closed his eyes, trying to imagine the sun upon his face, warm and rejuvenating.

"Far-Shooting Apollo... Lady Venus... Epona, mother of our camp..." He breathed deeply and calmed himself. "I have stepped into the unknown against your warnings. I know you cannot aid me on this quest, but I also know that you would not, nor ever have, punished me for fighting for what I believe in. It is not my intent to defy you with this quest, but to honour a friend who has saved my life, to help him regain his kingdom."

Lucius opened his eyes and tilted the amphora, emptying its entire contents onto the top of the altar before placing the jug in the carved bowl.

"Accept my offering that I may return home alive to my family, that they are kept safe in my absence. Give us strength on this journey, Gods, and know that I honour you."

Lucius bowed his head and began to back away to where Lunaris stood looking at him now. But he stopped, and went back.

"Mars, God of Battles and of the Earth, I know you do not always smile upon me, but here in this place, Romans heaped offerings in your name...may they walk in Elysium always." Lucius took the dagger from his cingulum then and held his hand over the altar. "To you, Mars, I offer my blood in this place..."

Lucius drew the dagger across his palm so that a sharp red line formed immediately and began to drip onto stone to mingle with the wine of his offering. "Give me strength in the battle to come..."

A rustling at the back of the courtyard made Lucius look up quickly and there, hidden amid a tangle of thick vines and thorns, a pair of eyes stared out at him.

It was the nymph.

Lucius stepped forward slowly, seeing her shudder.

"I won't hurt you," he said. "Are you all right? Why was he hunting you?"

The nymph calmed at his voice then, and emerged from the growth as if she were one with it, the thorns leaving her tunic and white skin unmolested.

"It is ever his sport to take us to his realm," she said. "Especially with the feast of Samhain upon us."

Lucius' mind raced. *This nymph knows him!* "Does he have any weaknesses?" he asked

She shook her head. "None. You cannot defeat him...Dragon." She pointed at his chest and the brilliant image of the dragon. "Even you..."

"Every man has a weakness."

"He is no man. He is not of this world," she said, stepping forward, close to Lucius now, her hand reaching up to almost brush his lips. "He is the Hunter. Beware his traps..."

She made to speak again, but at that moment Einion called from down the street.

"Lucius! We must move!"

The nymph shook her head and began to back away, her hand reaching behind her for the vines and briars until her skin melded into them and she disappeared once more.

Lucius stared at the spot for a moment and then looked to see the crows take flight into the grey sky where the wind was once more baring its teeth.

V

TERRAE MORTUAE

'The Dying Lands'

They left the final remnants of Rome's boot print far behind them, their mounts taking them over downs, across heathland, and around bogs and marshes, the land climbing and falling away intermittently. The lands through which they plodded, soaked and alert, grew more and more desolate and hostile.

The rough beauty of the place was not lost on Lucius, but it was hard to imagine this land sunlit and lively from beneath the dripping hem of his cloak's hood.

As ever, Einion rode in front, with Lucius and Dagon following side by side behind him.

They had long-ago exceeded the reach of Rome's roads, and so they now followed ancient trackways that seemed as old as the Gods themselves. At night they camped in the open, or beneath titanic, weathered rock formations, barely sleeping around a large fire.

They had seen nothing of Einion's people, and he began to wonder if they had all been wiped out in the plague Flaccus had told them about in Isca.

Lucius and Dagon thought of that as well, but they were more concerned with the sounds they heard at night - sounds of distant wailing, of screeches, and deep rumbles, a sort of breathing that could be felt in the very rocks upon which they camped.

When there was a break in rain, and the wind died away, Lucius edged Lunaris forward to ride beside Einion.

"We need more information so we aren't going in blind, Einion. Is there anyone at all around here who might be able or willing to help us?" Lucius stared at the Briton as they rode, for a moment hardly recognizing him for the circles of worry beneath his eyes and the weight upon his shoulders which quite literally pressed down on him. "Einion!"

The Briton snapped out of his reverie and turned to look at Lucius. "There is a place, yes," he paused, seeming to go back in his memories, to search behind that creased brow. "There is a pool where a priestess used to dwell. She...she was kind to me and Briana when we escaped. She may still be there."

"Can she be trusted?" Dagon asked, riding close behind them.

"Yes," Einion said.

"What kind of priestess is she? Of which god?" Lucius asked, hoping she was not a priestess of this Gwyn ap Nudd whom Einion had spoken of.

"She's a water nymph, the guardian of a sacred pool."

In his mind, Einion was suddenly back there with Briana, shaking and full of fear and rage, the blood of their battle and flight still upon their faces and arms. He was in the house beside the sacred pool, warming by the fire as Briana told the priestess of their ordeal. *Yes, we can trust her,* he told himself. *We can trust her.*

Einion reined in beside a trickling river that wended its way from their position between two distant tors, one covered with shattered rock, the other with rough shrubs dotted with white flowers. He pointed to a spot in the middle of the downs.

"See that lake, the small one at the top of the larger body?"

"Yes," Lucius said. "I see it."

"She'll be there, the priestess. If anyone can help us here, she can."

The ride to the distant pool was much farther than it had appeared when they first spotted it. It was encouraging that, after a while, smoke could be seen spiralling up into the low clouds, indicating that someone was indeed there. Whether it was the priestess or not, they could only guess at.

There were no trees for miles it seemed, the land covered instead by boulders, bog moss and meadow grass of the deepest green Lucius had ever seen.

They turned off of the ancient trackway and down a rocky slope, following a new path cut by the rainwater. The ground rose on either side of them, hiding them from distant eyes, if there were any.

"The air smells tangy and sweet at once," Dagon said, pushing back his hood.

"It's the peat and the clover that surround the lake," Einion said, remembering it well. "And wait...do you hear that?"

"What?" Lucius asked.

Einion smiled. "Hooves."

Lucius and Dagon drew their blades immediately, but Einion shook his head. "Not of enemies," he said, still smiling. He pointed up to the ground on either side of them just as a herd of black, white and brown moor ponies charged past.

"Horses?" Dagon said with relief, having expected an enemy.

"Yes," Einion answered. "They run wild on the moors. They've always tended to gather around the sacred pool to run and eat the clover that covers the ground."

If only Phoebus and Calliope could see this now, Lucius thought as he watched the ponies jump, and charge, and play, their manes flowing wildly in the wet air.

The three riders emerged at the edge of the small lake which, it seemed, was protected by a wall of mist that rested around the edges.

"Will we be safe here?" Lucius asked, dismounting and stretching at the edge of the water. He scanned the area and could see a single roundhouse far to the left, set back from the edge of the lake on a patch of higher ground. "There's the smoke," he said. "Now where is the priestess?"

Just as he spoke, a massive horse, several hands taller than Lunaris appeared before them, between the three riders and the distant house.

"Where did he come from?" Dagon asked, looking up at the magnificent animal.

Lucius stepped forward and the stallion craned its neck to sniff and nudge him.

Lucius thought that Lunaris would have reared and nipped at the horse, but, on the contrary, he seemed as interested as Lucius, moving forward, his ears twitching, his head bobbing.

"He is the guardian of the herds here," a voice said from behind all of them.

The three men whipped around to see a tall woman in the white robes of a priestess. She had long black, braided hair down to her waist, and a black cloak that protected her from the elements, though she held her head and neck high and straight, as if the cold had no bearing upon her.

Einion stepped forward to meet her. "Hello, lady," he said.

The woman's watery blue eyes widened, and her face was a mixture of relief and sadness as she raised her pale hand to touch Einion's face.

"You've come back," she said.

He nodded. "Yes. The time has come."

"Has it been so long?" she said.

Einion said nothing, but nodded again before turning to his companions. "My friends, Lucius and Dagon." Einion bowed his head to the priestess. "This is Elana, priestess and guardian of the sacred pool."

Lucius and Dagon both inclined their heads out of respect to the woman who seemed to reflect light with every movement.

"The Gods welcome you here, though the homecoming in this sickened land may not be what you expect," she said to Einion.

"I expect blood alone," Einion said, his face darkening quickly.

"And you shall have it," she said, her eyes stormy in that moment. "But first, come, rest. Get you warm by the hearth and care for your mounts who have carried you far.

She turned and began walking back to her home, the giant horse following close behind her.

"How long have you known her?" Lucius whispered to Einion.

The Briton smiled. "A long time."

"She doesn't look that old," Dagon said, a little too loudly.

They could not see Elana smiling to herself as she led the way.

Inside the roundhouse, scattered lamps burned, giving it a warm, golden glow. A central hearth flickered brightly and without smoke, and the three men gathered around it, shedding their sodden cloaks.

The priestess went to a table where she poured boiled water into four cups and returned to give one to each of them before taking one herself.

Lucius felt exhaustion come over him, his lids heavy as he stared at the flames. His family came to mind then, a warm memory to drive the chill from his bones, and yet accompanied by a stab of fear. He tried to hide it, but noticed the priestess staring at him.

"Drink the tea," she said. "It will warm and rejuvenate you."

Einion had already drunk his, and Dagon and Lucius followed suit.

After several minutes, she brought them a platter of bread and cheese, and served them bowls of hot broth made with field greens.

Slowly they felt strength returning to their bodies and minds, and when she saw the transformation completed, Elana turned to Einion.

"Your coming is late," she said.

"I'm sorry. I... I was told the time was now...and I was-"

"He was helping me in the North," Lucius said, feeling partly responsible for the devastation they had heard of in that broad green land.

"It is not your fault, Dragon," she said, though not unkindly. "The Gods have their ways."

"Tell me what has happened in Dumnonia, Elana," Einion leaned forward and looked into the priestess' eyes. "I must know."

"These are the dying lands now," she said. "Since the murder of your father, and the flight of you and your sister, your uncle, Caradoc, has ravaged the land and its people. They are able to keep but a little of what they rear or grow, and since the pestilence, their strength has waned such that they cannot even farm or tend their flocks. The will to support a murderer and tyrant is just not there."

"My father was not so kind as all that," Einion said suddenly. "Why should the land thrive under his rule and not my uncle's?"

"Your father was unkind to you, perhaps, but to his people, he was a king." Her stare was harsh and uncompromising.

Einion's head bent beneath her gaze, and the weight of what she said pressed upon him. *My father never had time for me,* he thought. *He was always ruling his people. It was all for others.*

"I don't suppose I have any allies left in this land," Einion said. "Is everyone gone?"

"Do you think your people so weak? You are their rightful king!" Elana was standing now, her eyes sweeping the circle of fire where the three warriors sat, Einion ridden with guilt, and Lucius and Dagon unsure of her power. "How can you expect them to fight when you despair?"

"I am back now, and will do what I must for them," Einion said.

Dagon spoke up. "Has the pestilence not come to this lake?" he asked. "I see you are well, and the herds of horses about appear healthy. Surely there are other places such as this?"

61

"This lake is protected by the Gods," she said to the Sarmatian. "But even that protection is waning in the face of the crowding darkness sweeping through this land."

"Has the Hunter been here?" Lucius blurted out.

Elana wheeled on him, her next sentence choked back as she held her breath. "You speak his name so easily?"

"He is a man," Lucius lied.

"You are no fool, Dragon. And neither is the Lord of Annwn. To challenge him is death, and I have heard his hunting horn screaming over the moors these last three nights."

Einion was silent, frozen in thought.

"We saw him off," Dagon said.

She laughed. "You did not. He is waiting. He is the Hunter - patient and cunning. Skilled above all others at the kill. His horn heralds death."

"Then it will be his own," Lucius said.

At that moment, the flames leapt up to singe the beam crossing over the fire, and Lucius saw warriors led by Gwyn ap Nudd, horned and screaming, their horses charging across hill and dale. He heard the wail of women and children, the cries of men cut down, and -

"Stop this!" Lucius yelled.

The flames were low and the hearth calm. His friends stared at him in shock as he looked from one to the other of them, and then back at the priestess.

"What is it, Anguis?" Dagon said, his hand squeezing Lucius' forearm.

"I saw...in the flames, I saw..." He turned to Elana. "What did you do to me?"

"I did nothing," she said, her voice calm. "The veil is thinning, and Samhain draws near."

"I need air," Lucius said, getting up and going out the door into the dusk.

"I'll tend the horses," Dagon said, following Lucius with a backward glance at the priestess.

"Forgive them, Elana," Einion said. "They are men of war, and for them it is unthinkable to plan an attack without knowing where they are going. I've not had enough information to give them."

"You have been away for long, and your mind has stowed the painful memories of your past, Einion." She sat down beside him and put a hand on his arm, her voice soft and reassuring now after the previous harshness. "But you *are* king in these lands, no matter what Rome says."

"I will take the throne back," he said, his teeth gritted.

"First you must cross the moors, and to do this, you must pass through the worst part of the lands. I have mentioned the pestilence, but there is a terror between there and here, a menace upon the moors that is older than time."

"The wyrm?" he said. "I have heard of it."

"Some say it is a wyrm, but no one really knows. All that is certain is that any flocks, horses, or humans who reach the heart of the dying lands are never seen again. I believe that is why your uncle has remained safe, out of Rome's reach."

"And there has been no one to stand against him," Einion stood, as did she.

"Until now." At that moment, Elana took Einion's head in her hands and pulled him forward to kiss his forehead in blessing. "The gods and spirits of this land are with you in this, Einion. We all depend on you to heal this land."

Einion's face was awash with fury and sadness, as if all the emotion of the last twenty years had amassed in a swirling orb in the midst of his chest, disturbed with every breath, every step closer to his childhood home. He had been waiting for too long to unleash the fury caged inside, and soon the time would be at hand.

He kissed Elana's hands and touched them to his forehead. Then, he went outside to breathe the evening air.

A short distance away, Dagon was brushing down the horses, and directly ahead, Lucius stood at the edge of the small lake, gazing at the setting sun where it painted the sky in pink and orange to the West, just beyond the low green hills.

"When we fled and came to this place, I would stand in exactly this spot, every evening, and watch the sun set over the kingdom." Einion said to Lucius, staring at the horizon.

"It is beautiful," Lucius said. "There is something about this place..." He breathed deeply and stared at the muddy shore.

"What did you see in the fire?" Einion asked.

Lucius shook his head. "The Hunter. Many hunters. I've never seen anything like it." A chill ran up Lucius' spine and he reached for the hilt of his sword.

"At Samhain the dead go on the hunt across the land. The Lord of Annwn leads them."

Lucius looked at the Briton, doubt upon his face, but inside he felt terror pulling at him. *I've never fought an enemy like this,* he thought. *Apollo...I know you warned me. Forgive me, but the die is cast.*

"I tell you this, Lucius," Einion said. "When we left this sacred place and went to the Romans for help, we got none. Even though our cause was just. But you are here, despite the danger." He paused, stifling a chill of dread. "I will never forget this, and neither should you, my friend." He put his hand upon Lucius' shoulder, but the latter only nodded.

"I'll go help Dagon," Einion said when Lucius did not answer. "He *is* a king after all, and my test is yet to come."

Lucius watched Einion go to Dagon and help finish brushing down the horses.

Dagon had just finished with Lunaris and let him go.

Immediately, the dapple grey stallion trotted over to Lucius and stood beside him, leaned into him.

"My friend," Lucius said. "We'll get through this. It's just another battle."

Lunaris waved his great mane and bent over to drink from the water. When he rose again, Lucius put his arms around the stallion's neck and felt the heat coming off of his soft coat, hid behind the long strands of his black mane, until he heard footsteps coming out of the roundhouse.

"He is supremely loyal to you," Elana said. "They are magnificent creatures." Her blue eyes stared across the lake to the horses running to and fro on the other side, splashing along the shoreline and running up and down the green embankments that hid the sacred pool from the outside world.

The priestess continued. "Our returning king carries a heavy burden, for which he is fortunate to have you and the Sarmatian with him."

"He is our friend and ally," Lucius said, his voice harsher than he intended.

"You also have your own burdens to carry, Dragon," she said. "I cannot tell you what I sense or see, for the Gods have not always played fair with me."

Lucius looked up at her then, and she seemed less powerful than before, the veil of power falling away briefly to reveal the frailty beneath.

"Are you not a nymph?" he asked.

"Of a sort, yes. But I am no goddess."

"And I am no god," Lucius added. "How then do I fight one?"

"I do not know," she said. "But this much I can see, Lucius Metellus Anguis - you are indeed blessed by the Gods, and though they cannot help you in this fight, they are with you."

She reached up and pat Lunaris' strong neck, her fingers shaking a little as she did so. Lucius did not see the single tear that ran down her cheek to be lost in the folds of her black cloak.

Just then, the last light of the sun fell away behind the hills, and darkness swept in around them.

They did not hear the hunting horn of the Lord of Annwn that night, for the mists guarded the sacred pool well in the pitch and silvery night. Lucius, Einion and Dagon slept soundly,

65

aided by the priestess' tea, but they awoke with the dawn to eat, resupply, and saddle their horses.

Unknown to them, Elana had spent the night in vigil, beside the flames of the hearth fire, praying to the Gods for the protection of the triad of would-be heroes lying beneath her roof, and for the deliverance of the land of which she was a part, as much as any wild horse, towering elm, or delicate clover.

It was not raining, and the sun's morning light lit the sacred pool with gold, the mist hovering over it and amid the herds of ponies who came to drink at the shore.

"The mist extends far onto the moors today - it will cloak your approach," she said to the three of them. She walked up to Dagon first. "You are without lands, but I can see that you are a true king, loved by your people. Know that you are close to finding a home once more."

"Thank you," Dagon said to her, his head high, his hand upon his horse.

"And you, Lucius Metellus Anguis..." she said, standing before Lucius. "My word cannot counter that of the Gods, but I would say that inside, you know where your loyalties lie. I also know that this land needs you far more than you know." She said no more to Lucius, but reached out and stroked Lunaris' forehead, muttering some words that none of them fully comprehended.

She then turned to Einion.

"You know your task. You are the rightful lord of this land," she said, gazing down at the sword that had belonged to his father. "I was there when that sword was bestowed upon your father, and I would also be there when you rest safely upon his throne." Elana turned to a boulder nearby where a small dish of shell rested. Inside there was what appeared to be blood, and she dipped three fingers into it. Then, her eyes locked onto Einion's, and she ran her fingers across his forehead. "May the Gods guide your sword, and grant you the reclamation of your throne, and the healing of this land. Go now."

Einion did not speak, for he was loathe to leave the peace of that place, the first steps out of it always the most difficult, the first steps toward certain danger.

When they were all mounted, they nudged their horses and led them up the small path, away from the sacred pool, and back to the ancient track. None of them spoke for some time.

The mist clung to the land as they rode, but the forms of giant tors could be spotted, rising out of the ground like Titans slowly breaking free of the depths of Tartarus. Some were brown and rough, others green, and others smooth and grey, glistening with morning dew and mist.

Eventually, Einion spoke up.

"We're about a day's ride from the fortress," he said. "We need to stop for the night."

"Where can we stop around here?" Dagon asked, as Lucius passed them both and scanned the wide, ancient moor before them.

"I know of a place," Einion said, his voice a little far off before he spoke louder. "It is isolated."

"Are there any villages on the way?" Lucius asked, wary now of enemies so close to Einion's ancestral home.

"There is one," he answered. "But there is no way around it." He pulled his hood over his head and urged his mount forward onto a muddy road that swept away from them, toward the downs.

As they rode, a massive tor rose up on their right, the boulders like flattened discs that threatened to slide off one another and crush them as they passed. The wind picked up, and set the rock formations to humming around them.

"Does anyone live in those rocks?" Dagon asked, his sword drawn as he looked up at the formations.

"No. No one mortal, anyway," Einion said, looking back and smiling.

"I'm glad you're joking," Lucius said. "But it does feel like we're being watched." He too drew his sword.

They came to a tall standing stone that loomed beside the trackway and aligned with another in the distance.

"This road has been in use since long before Rome was born," Einion said.

Lucius nodded and looked to the left where another tor rose up, this one rocky and green. Still, there were no signs of life, or of death in that place.

"The village is on the slopes of the next tor," Einion said as the passage narrowed into a defile and they rode one in front of the other.

Ahead, on the right, rose a rocky brown tor where a gathering of squat stone structures huddled in a close group, as if to hide from the elements that no doubt pounded that place.

"I see some movement," Dagon said, his hand shielding his eyes from the light mist that was falling now. "You should get behind us so no one recognizes you," he told Einion.

Einion nodded and dropped back, putting Lucius and Dagon between him and the village on their right.

There was a faint moan on the air and several forms emerged from the stone hovels to shamble down the hillside toward the riders. They were covered in rags and their arms were outstretched toward the strangers. Soon enough, a group of about twenty men, women and children were gathered on the road, blocking the way, every one of them with their hands out, their voices pleading and pitiful.

As they came closer, Lucius could see the red and black blotches covering their skin, the broken pustules upon their faces and hands.

"Are they lepers?" Dagon said, his sword out toward them as they came closer and closer.

"Don't hurt them," Einion said.

"Not them I'm worried about," Dagon answered, but put up his sword.

"Please help us!" a woman cried, holding the body of a dead infant whose skin had turned as black as if it had come out of the ashes of a fire.

Lucius held his breath as the smell careened with his senses, as if they had ridden into a wall of decay.

It seemed that each person was sicker than the last, those who were less sick having had the strength to push their way to the front of the small mob.

"Stay back!" Lucius said, the fear of plague overcoming him for a moment. "We mean you no harm!"

"Let us pass!" Dagon said.

Beneath the cowl of his cloak, Einion's eyes were wide and watery. The state of his people's lives was like a dagger to his gut then, and he knew he had let them down waiting so long to return. He had failed his family, his duty, by not killing his uncle on the day of his attack at Samhain, so many years ago.

At the back of the crowd, a lone person stood still and silent, simply watching the three men pass. Whether it was a man or a women, Einion could not tell, but he spotted the eyes beneath the hood staring at him, boring into him. He looked away, the urge to vomit too great as a man with a bloody, maggoty stub of an arm waved the appendage in his direction.

They all wept, and cried, and stank - a great mass of rotting life. After a few minutes, the group morphed into a single decrepit entity that the three men simply wanted to get away from, so once they were past the final person on the road, they kicked their horses hard, leaving the dismal keening behind them for a time.

"What could have done that to those people?" Dagon asked. "I've never seen a sickness like that."

Lucius shook his head, still sweating from the encounter, but Einion spoke up.

"When the land dies, so do the people." *I just hope I'm not too late...*

They passed two more such villages within the next couple of hours before they came onto a wide open moor where the ancient highway was marked by standing stones stretching out before them.

The clouds rested much higher in the air, giving the land a much more open, lonely aspect.

Their horses trotted over the damp, green ground, following the line of the road and ancient stones.

"This moor used to be full of grazing sheep and moor ponies, and covered with wildflowers," Einion said, shaking his head so that his long hair wavered from one side to the other. "I can't believe this is the same place."

"I'm sure those villagers back there think the same," Lucius said. He covered his mouth and nose and gasped. "Did it always smell like this?"

"No," Einion answered.

"Smells like the mud pools in Numidia, don't you think, Lucius?" Dagon said.

"Aye. Maybe worse though." Lucius pointed. "What's that structure over there?"

They looked to the North, and in the middle of the moor was a green mound surrounded by what seemed to be walls.

"That's where we're going to spend the night," Einion said. "It's the safest place around here." He kicked his horse and they carried on.

To Lucius, it was a place of memory. There did not seem to be that feeling of eyes upon them, but something else, something as old as the Gods themselves. He drew his sword from his back and kicked Lunaris forward, but as they got nearer to the structure, the stallion shied and fought Lucius.

"Hey, what is it, boy? You should be happy. Look at all that green grass you can eat."

Lunaris continued to shy, but Lucius was firm on the reins and urged him forward after the other mounts who were also displaying similar behaviour.

"The horses are not happy," Dagon said out loud. "Maybe we should press on?"

"There is nowhere else to go," Einion said, dismounting before the structure and pulling on his mount's reins. "This is the last stop before we reach the fortress. We need to plan and strike out from here."

The horses finally relented and moved through a narrow opening at one end of the rectangular structure. High stone panels were closely fitted around the perimeter, forming solid walls, large enough to shield men and horses from the winds that ravaged the landscape. Grass sprouted from the bottom of each stone panel, as if each had grown out of the earth in some forgotten age.

Lucius wondered if the Titans had travelled this far in ages past.

"What is this place?" Dagon asked.

"It's a hunting lodge. My ancestors have used it for as long as I can remember," Einion said. "I've spent many a night here with friends in my youth, when we were hunting boar, deer, or rabbits on the moors. On a clear night, the heavens themselves light the interior as if a fire were kindled in our midst."

"It's as good a place as any," Lucius said. "Let's unsaddle the horses and let them graze before it gets dark."

The three of them set to, and Einion lit a fire in the central pit of the ancient lodge, in a spot that was dark with age, but seemed not to have seen fire for some time.

As twilight settled over the moors, they hunkered down for a night of intermittent rain. The three men sat around the fire, going over their options, while the horses fidgeted in one of the corners of the lodge. The firelight cast its glow on the stone walls, highlighting small, crystalline specs in the stone.

Lucius thought that were it not for the severity of their quest, it would have been a nice place to come hunting.

"What are the approaches to the fortress?" Dagon asked Einion, his sharpening stone running the length of his sword as he spoke.

"They are few," Einion began. "The castle is upon a rock jutting out into the sea, and the only way in is across the causeway to the south, part of which is a rope bridge."

"How far is the drop?" Lucius asked. "Are the seaside cliffs shear?"

Einion looked at him. "If anyone fell from those heights, their bones would shatter upon the rocks on the one side, or be tossed and broken by the raging seas on the other." He leaned back, as if fully realizing the task ahead of them. "The only way is through the front gates, and to do that, we'll need to sneak in somehow."

"Under cover of night?" Lucius said. "We could disarm the guards. There are so few people around here, it may be that your uncle does not place a heavy guard on the gates?"

"I wouldn't bet on it."

"What would he do if you challenged him to single combat?" Dagon said. "In my country, single combat is witnessed by the Gods, and no ruler would ever think of refusing."

Einion laughed coldly. "My uncle has no honour. He would as soon stick a knife in my back without even hearing what I had to say. He can't be trusted."

"Which means there are no behaviours we can rely upon to plan something," Lucius said. "I hate to say this, Einion, but this is going to be harder than we thought. Unless we can get in there, you won't be able to kill him."

Einion was silent, his eyes cold and angry as he stared into the flames before him. "Gods!" he said, pounding the soft earth with his fist and getting up.

Dagon made to go after him, but Lucius held him back.

"Let him go. He needs to think this through. Only he can devise a way to get inside, and he hasn't been there in years."

"The Gods do challenge him with this task," Dagon said. "For myself, I have no kingdom to reclaim, but for him, it is there for the taking."

"Except he has an army of three," Lucius said grimly.

Dagon stared back at him and nodded. "We've faced worse odds."

"I don't know about that. Depends on how many men his uncle has." Lucius ate a last piece of dried meat and stood to stretch and look up at the sky. Stars winked and were veiled before their eyes, and the near-full moon lit the heavens in silver before banks of cloud rushed in to block the way. "Gods, I hope you can see us here," Lucius whispered, and Dagon, having heard him, echoed the sentiment.

Lunaris whinnied and thrashed at the other end of the lodge then, and Lucius went over to calm him.

"Easy, boy! What don't you like about this place?" He stroked the stallion's dappled coat and felt the horse shudder. Lucius turned to Dagon who knew more about horses than he ever would. "What's wrong with him? All of them? They're all shaking."

Dagon came over to his own mount and spoke soothing words in his Sarmatian tongue. The horse tossed its head and stomped its thick hooves in the mud, while Einion's smaller mount did likewise, pulling at the rope like a skittish lamb being led to slaughter.

"Pah! What is that smell? How could he live in a place like this?" Dagon said, covering his mouth.

"Smell shouldn't affect the horses so much," Lucius said.

They both looked up at each other in that instant, eyes wide.

"Einion!"

It felt good to be on the moor again, and Einion revisited myriad childhood memories in that place as he stood there looking up at the wide, dark sky and the waxing moon where it burned behind the windswept clouds like lanterns in a gale. *Were it not for the smell of this place, I would make it my home,* he thought.

He had walked some distance from the lodge, angry with himself and their situation. He knew he had betrayed his friends by leading them there without a solid plan. Etain had told him to trust in the Gods' wisdom, but he had seen little sign of the Gods since entering Dumnonia. They seemed to have abandoned the land as surely as he had.

He unsheathed his father's sword and held it out before him in the moonlight so that the blade gleamed cold and bright, and his warlike shadow was cast upon the sodden ground.

He had a sudden urge to vomit for the stench about him had become unbearable. His eyes closed for a moment against the urge, and he opened them to see his shadow changed, malformed. It confused him for a moment.

"Einion!" Lucius' voice called from the entrance to the hunting lodge. "Look out!"

Einion wheeled around only just as a hideous mouth with enormous fangs reared over him and dove downward to engulf him.

He jumped and rolled, and slashed out with his blade to slam into something as hard as rock.

The wyrm!

The beast reared above him, coiled, ready to strike again. It was true, the beast existed, the bane of his people.

"Sarmatiana!" Dagon cried as he arrived at a run, leaping over the beast's thrashing tail and hacking into it as he passed.

Einion saw his chance, but as he moved in, the wyrm turned on Dagon and the great tail swept him at the legs, sending him flying through the air to land against one of the standing stones on the ancient track.

Apollo guide me, Lucius prayed as he rushed in to help Dagon now, visions of his god and the great Python flashing in the back of his mind. *Was it as big as this monster?*

From the side, the wyrm seemed as long as thirty feet, and thick as a tree. Its skin was armoured, scaled in smooth black and deepest green that would have been beautiful to look upon were it not for the terror it inspired.

Lucius dove in and stabbed, the beast turning on him now, lunging at him, the great dripping fangs missing him only by inches.

Dagon attacked again, and then Lucius, but their attacks seemed to have little effect.

There was only anger and hunger in those great yellow eyes, the slits narrowing before each attack, widening with each cut, and still it did not slow.

Lucius tripped backward and thought the end was upon him for a moment before Dagon leaped upon the wyrm's back and plunged one of his daggers into its side.

The thing thrashed and roared, a sound they could only bear by covering their ears in desperation.

Lucius watched in horror as Dagon was thrown through the air, several feet away, only to be pursued by the wyrm as it slithered through the grass toward its prey.

"Dagon!" Lucius found his feet and ran as fast as he could, leaping and pinning the beast's tail to the ground with his sword, and holding fast to the handle, as if holding a planted spear in the face of a cavalry charge.

The wyrm soared over him and was ready to fall upon him when suddenly a flash of grey and white appeared between them.

Lunaris reared and kicked at the wyrm's face, his black mane and tail flying like angry flames in the wind as he protected Lucius, tapping into realms of aggression that he had never explored upon the battlefield. His powerful, flailing hooves fended off several attacks, dealing several blows to the wyrm's eyes and snapping one of the deathly fangs with a horrific crack.

Lunaris stood and reared again, his battle cry more like that of a chimera's as he prepared for another assault.

"No!" Lucius yelled, watching as the stallion landed another kick in the wyrm's eyes.

The dread wyrm pulled back, shaking its black head in pain and anger, and then returned full of fury to sink its great fangs into Lunaris' belly.

"NO!!!" Lucius cried again, wrenching his sword free of the ground and running in, even as Lunaris' screams rent the air and blood showered over him.

The wyrm shook its great head again, nostrils flaring, eyes like yellow fire as it savaged the horse and then tossed the body away.

Lucius lunged and plunged his sword into the side of the beast's head, but it glanced off and he fell into the puddle of blood below, on top of Lunaris' convulsing body.

The wyrm reared and hissed again, its aspect horrible against the light of the moon, and made to finish the man before him.

Gods watch over my family for me, Lucius said at the back of his mind.

The beast struck like a giant viper and Lucius felt the shadow of the jaws enclose him and Lunaris, even as someone else appeared at his side and the fangs stuck in the ground around them.

Einion crouched beside Lucius in that dark hole of death and glistening fangs, his father's sword stuck deep in the roof of the wyrm's mouth, planted in the thing's brain.

On the outside, Dagon straddled the shuddering body, his own sword up to the hilt, wedged between black scales above the spine.

"Anguis!" Dagon's exhausted voice called out. "Anguis!"

The stench was overwhelming in the jaws, and Lucius and Einion fell into unconsciousness, as if plunged into an abyss on the road to Tartarus itself.

VI

PESTIS POPULUS

'People of the Plague'

It was a sickly cracking and prying that woke Lucius up. The darkness was lightened by grey light filtering in through small gaps in the black and stinking walls about him. More and more light assaulted his eyes, and someone beside him began to moan.

Einion!

Before Lucius could speak, he remembered the horrors of the previous night and felt his body shudder where it lay hunched over Lunaris' massacred form.

There, his face buried in the bloody coat of his horse, Lucius wept, the convulsions stronger and more desperate for all the grief that now washed over him.

He could feel the light spreading around him now, but he did not care. Lunaris was dead, he who had carried Lucius into countless battles. They had travelled the empire together, and it was here on this remote and stinking moor that the noble stallion had met his end. *Defending me!* Lucius cried.

"Einion?" Lucius said, his hand reaching out but meeting nothing.

"Stay back!" Dagon's voice, and the urgency with which he uttered his threats, suddenly slapped Lucius out of his remorse and he turned to look.

The body of the wyrm had been hacked with an axe and its cave-like jaws peeled away from them. A great circle of blood radiated from them, and beyond the stained earth stood a mass of plague-people staring at them and trying to move closer to Lucius and Einion, but held at bay by Dagon whose long sword slashed the air between them.

"Anyone who comes close dies!" the Sarmatian king said, his armour and clothes sticky with blood.

Lucius pushed himself to his feet and picked up his sword to stumble to Dagon's side.

"We only want to help," one of them said. "You've rid us of the terror of the moors."

"We will cut each of you down if you come closer!" Lucius said, shaking his head and feeling a wave of nausea come over him. "Stay back!"

Einion was standing now, behind Lucius and Dagon, limping from a cut to his thigh where the wyrm's fang had grazed him.

"You need help!" said a woman who stepped forward.

"You're sick!" Dagon said to her.

The woman thrust back her cowl and stepped forward. "No. We're not!"

Dagon's blade was raised, overcome as he was by fury and death that he would have cut her down were it not for Einion's strong grip.

"Dagon no!" Einion yelled, pulling the Sarmatian backward, his hands shaking. "I...I...know her."

Einion turned to face the woman, but did not step closer. He squinted as if through a haze and then gasped.

"Gwendolyn?"

The woman stood still, relief and amazement showing on her ravaged face.

"You've come back?"

Einion was about to rush forward, but Lucius grabbed him. "She's diseased, Einion! Don't!"

"No. I'm not," she said, taking a cloth from her satchel and running it across the purple and black blotches marring her skin to reveal the white of her face beneath. "I am not. None of us are," she said, taking a step closer. "You've come back." Her voice shook this time and she reached out.

"You're alive?" Einion's voice was a throaty whisper, and in a moment he was grasping her close as if he had not seen her for lifetimes.

Lucius and Dagon stood there behind them, watching as every other villager did the same and wiped away the artifice of their sores.

"Our rightful lord has returned!" an older man called out from their midst, and some of the people wept and reached out to touch Einion's bloody arms, shoulders and hair before thanking the other two warriors who had accompanied him.

"And he has brought a dragon with him to help us!" cried another.

The mass of villagers turned to face Lucius, some pointing at the gore-encrusted dragon upon his chest.

He did not hear the thanks, the praise, or feel their hands reaching out to touch the image of the dragon upon his armour. The ringing in his head had grown too loud, and the corpse behind him pulled at his heart such that he could think of nothing else.

Lucius turned away from the people around him, and went over to Lunaris. Never would he have thought such a thing would have been possible. He felt Dagon's hand upon his shoulder, and the whispered words of parting and peace that the Sarmatians uttered whenever one of their horses left for the grassy seas of the Afterlife.

"I've never seen a horse fight so fiercely," Dagon said. "We will remember him always."

"I have to burn him," Lucius said numbly. "I can't leave him here beside this thing!" He spat at the wyrm's body.

"You can't burn him," the woman said from behind them.

Lucius turned, fury in his eyes, to face Einion and Gwendolyn.

"What do you mean, I can't burn him? I'll give him the honour he deserves!"

Einion held up his hand and put it against Lucius' chest, the latter glaring at him so fiercely that Dagon had to step in.

"She's right, Lucius," Einion said, more calmly. "We're too close to the fortress now. If we make a pyre, it will alert my uncle's men."

"Caradoc does not often leave the stronghold, but if such a fire were to burn, he would send scouts," Gwendolyn said.

Lucius balled his fists, seeing the right of what they were saying, and hating it. "Gods!" He knelt beside Lunaris' head and placed his shaking hand upon the stallion's cold cheek. *He was so full of life and warmth a short time ago...*

He knew he should be used to death, but some were more difficult to bear than others. *First Alerio, now you. Britannia has brought us only death.*

"Anguis," Dagon's voice, as always, cut through his despair and rallied him like a strong wind in a drifting ship's sails. "They are right. We can't afford for the enemy to know we're here."

"But his spirit will not be set free," Lucius said.

"Epona will see him cared for, I've no doubt." Dagon pulled Lucius up.

"You're right," Lucius said, turning to Einion and Gwendolyn. "The fire would attract the enemy. But how do we know none of you will alert Einion's uncle?"

The woman stared straight at Lucius, unafraid after so much fear. "You haven't lived in this land since the king was murdered. You wouldn't say such things if you knew what we have gone through. Caradoc is an animal, a tyrant. The wyrm took all of our livestock, and some of our children. And then there were the disappearances in the dark of night. You don't know, Dragon. You can't."

Lucius stared back at her, this dark version of Briana, and nodded. "Forgive me. My grief clouds my mind."

Just then, Einion stumbled to the ground, sweating, and grasping at his leg.

"Einion!" Gwendolyn said, on her knees beside him.

"The wyrm's fang grazed him," Lucius said.

"We have to get him to our village. Quickly!" she told the villagers. Some came forward to lift Einion, as Lucius and Dagon gathered their things and the other two horses from inside the hunting lodge.

As Lucius pulled Einion's horse by the reins, the animal carrying his own saddlebags as well now, he paused at the tail end of the file of pseudo plague victims, and stared back at the place of the massacre. It began to rain again, and the blood gathered in pools about the bodies.

The downpour washed Lunaris as it came down, revealing the brilliant, dappled coat and the angry gashes and fang holes that had allowed the life to leach out of him.

The woman, Gwendolyn, came over to Lucius when he and Dagon emerged from the hunting lodge. "You should bring all your horse's harness and saddle with you."

"What?" Lucius said, his anger returning.

"If Caradoc's men find Roman harness and saddlery here, it will raise suspicion. It may alert him to something."

"You don't even know why we're here," Lucius said.

Gwendolyn looked back to where Einion was. "I think I do," she said before going back to Einion's side as the group set out.

Lucius stared up at the sky and closed his eyes. *Epona...Goddess...please watch over him. Guide him to the Afterlife.*

He then removed the harness from Lunaris' body, fetched the saddle from inside the lodge, and turned to join Dagon and the others who were already following one of the ancient trackways leading to the northwest.

How long they walked, Lucius did not know, for in that land, it seemed that time had no meaning, the sun no presence. All he could surmise was that they were making their way toward a great steep tor of grey rock, and the closer they got, the more visible became the gathering of squat stone houses about its base, built so as to blend in with the hill itself.

They passed rotting corpses on the way, and piles of bones, the flesh of which had been cleaned off, leaving them white and grey upon the muddy ground.

Lucius and Dagon exchanged looks.

"Victims from other villages," one of the old women near them said from beneath her torn, black shawl. "Gwendolyn ordered them scattered about to keep Caradoc's people away from our homes."

"Good thing," said another woman. "Else Caradoc would come here every moon to take what little food we have. It's bad enough he is forcing us to honour him at Samhain two nights hence with offerings."

"Then Gwendolyn is your leader?" Lucius asked.

The woman nodded. "She is our rock and saviour in this gods-forsaken place. Our elders were slain when they stood up to Caradoc."

An old man Lucius presumed to be the woman's husband, spoke next. "When she arrived at our village, days after the massacre, she got us organized, and took us into hiding."

Lucius and Dagon nodded and gazed ahead to where Gwendolyn walked beside the cart that carried Einion.

"I hope he's all right," Dagon said "Otherwise, this is wasted."

"He'll pull through," Lucius said. "He has to."

They approached the village where a sign said 'Plague', in Dumnonian.

They passed beneath an archway where more bones and the bodies of crows swung in the breeze.

"Get him inside my home!" Gwendolyn said to the men who brought Einion down off the cart as he mumbled. She then turned to Lucius and Dagon and pointed to another outbuilding several meters away. "You can stable the horses in there." She followed Einion quickly, leaving Lucius and Dagon standing there in the middle of the small, muddy, bone-strewn village.

They led the horses to the building Gwendolyn had shown them, unsaddled them, and carried all of the saddle bags and weapons to the house where Einion lay upon a table as his leg was probed and washed.

"The leather of his breeches prevented the fang from sinking too deep and into his bone," Gwendolyn said as she bent over Einion, the latter held down by two of the older men. "But there is a piece of leather in there that I have to..." There was a loud sucking sound and then, "...get out!" Gwendolyn held the probe up and showed them the piece of bloody leather. "Help me now," she said to Lucius and Dagon as she took a small amphora of wine off a shelf. "Hold him down," she ordered.

Lucius and Dagon stepped forward and pinned Einion's arms and legs.

"Easy brother," Lucius whispered. "You seem to be in good hands."

Gwendolyn looked at Lucius and nodded. "Ready?"

He nodded.

She poured, and immediately, Einion's limbs went rigid as if a great pain laced his entire body. "Hold him!" she said, pouring more wine before taking a liberal pinch of herbs from a nearby jar and plunging them into the wound left by the wyrm's fang.

Einion's body continued to shake for some time, but he eventually tired of fighting and went limp.

"How do you know what to do?" Lucius asked as Gwendolyn bandaged Einion's thigh with linen.

"We've had to deal with a few wounds from that beast, a very few from people who survived an attack. Most were killed and devoured..." she choked back tears now that her work was done and she could let her guard down. "There are many plants and herbs upon the moors that fight such poisons."

"It's good you came upon us then," Dagon said.

She looked up at them but did not say anything, moving instead to build up the central hearth nearby. "Are either of you wounded?" she asked.

Dagon answered that he was well, but Lucius stared into the growing flames, his thoughts back on the moor, and going over the longer list of things he could have lost that day were it not for Lunaris' courage.

Night fell outside on the moors, and the driving rain gave way to a great jaundiced moon as Lucius and Dagon ate some broth and hard bread that Gwendolyn had given them.

They watched and waited as the woman tended Einion, never leaving his side, stroking his sweating forehead and pouring drops of water down his muttering lips.

"How long will he be like this?" Lucius asked her.

"Wyrm fever acts quickly. If he survives the night, then tomorrow he should wake up."

"And if not?" Dagon asked.

"Then this land is doomed." She bent to inspect the bandages.

Dagon leaned close to Lucius. "What do we do if...if he doesn't make it?"

"I don't know. We've come all this way," Lucius went over the possibility in his mind and could not accept it. Einion had become a part of the family as much as Dagon. He had put his own dreams of reclaiming his kingdom on hold so that he could help Lucius, and now, on the brink of making that dream a reality, he lay on the edge of oblivion.

"He's got to come through this," Lucius said, as if he intended Einion to take note.

"You should both sleep," Gwendolyn told them. "You have fought and suffered as well, and the mind must heal as much as the body." She walked across the flagstone floor, took two blankets from a stone shelf, and placed them on two cots.

"You can rest safely here," she reassured them. "Please."

Dagon looked at the cot and then to Lucius. "I could use some rest. Couldn't you?"

"I can try," Lucius answered, nodding his thanks to Gwendolyn. He walked over to the cot, unstrapped his sword, unbuckled his cuirass, and then laid it on the ground beside his saddlebags nearby. The sword, he kept beside him.

Dagon followed suit, and soon he was sleeping soundly beneath the thin coverlet Gwendolyn had given them.

It took some time for Lucius to fall asleep. His mind tortured him with repeated images of Lunaris in the maw of the wyrm upon the moor. He opened his eyes in frustration, forced himself to remain still, and looked across the dank dwelling to Gwendolyn where she stood over Einion.

She spoke in hushed tones to his prostrate friend, but Lucius could not hear what she said, though the glistening streams of tears running down her cheeks did not escape his notice. Her long, straight black hair hid most of her features. Gwendolyn was tall for a woman, her skin pale, no doubt due to the lack of sun in that land, and their hiding indoors. She was like Briana in many ways, and Lucius wondered if they were cousins, but by the way Gwendolyn cared for Einion, he suspected not. Her grey eyes turned toward him suddenly and Lucius felt a little ashamed at being caught staring at her.

He swung his legs over the edge of the cot and walked to her side.

"I am sorry about your horse," she said in a low voice.

Lucius nodded, still feeling numb to that particular reality. "Lunaris had been with me through many battles, in Numidia, and in Caledonia."

Gwendolyn looked back at Lucius' blood-encrusted armour. "You are the Dragon, the one we have heard tell of."

"I suppose I am. Though my men are as much dragons as I am."

"They are loyal?"

Lucius remembered the great oak tree, hung with the bodies of his horse warriors. "To the death," he said.

85

"Did Einion fight with you in the North?" she asked, kneeling beside him.

"He and Briana saved my life," Lucius said, "The Gods sent them to me to help protect my family."

"Where is Briana?" Gwendolyn asked excitedly. "She lives?"

"Yes. She wanted to come, but she agreed to stay and protect my family while I am here."

"Why does a Roman's family need protection?"

"You ask strange questions," Lucius said sadly.

"Do I? I thought it a good question. Romans rule the world, or most of it now, so why would you fear threats from those you have defeated?"

"It's not always Britons or Caledonians who threaten us."

"Your own people?"

"Yes. The worst of them." Lucius suddenly worried for Adara and the children.

Gwendolyn put her hand upon his arm and squeezed. "I suppose we understand that here too," she said, looking down at Einion.

Lucius said nothing for a moment, then spoke. "Does Einion's uncle, this Caradoc, have many men?"

"Yes," she said. "At least enough to keep us from trying to get at him."

"The villagers?" Lucius asked.

"When people suffer, they are willing to risk much against great odds to overthrow a tyrant."

"But not that much," Lucius added.

"No." She shook her head. "Not that much."

Lucius knelt beside Einion and took his hand, grateful that it was warm. "Tell me, Gwendolyn," he began. "Are the people truly loyal to Einion? Would they fight for him if the need arose?"

She took a deep breath before answering, her long neck straight and proud. "Those who are not sick...yes. They would."

"Good," Lucius said as he stood again. "I'll try and sleep now."

Before he reached the cot, Gwendolyn spoke. "Did he ever speak of me to you?"

Lucius shook his head. "No."

She sank a little in the spirits, but Lucius stepped toward her slowly. "But," he began, "he never speaks of Dumnonia, and only on the way here did he tell us exactly what happened. I could see that he was thinking of something, or someone, intently the entire journey here." Lucius tried to smile, as hard as it was. "Now I feel certain he was thinking of you."

Gwendolyn looked up from the floor, her grey eyes suddenly more hopeful than they had been since she found them upon the bloody moor.

"Let him hear your voice," Lucius said. "It will reach him and give him something to fight for."

Einion stood upon a shingle beach, the sea crashing before him, its spray wetting his face as he gazed up toward the massif that had been his home. There were screams from within, like the cries of deathly gulls overhead, and blood ran in rivulets over the edges of the rocks, just as it did when a tempest pounded the fortress.

In his hand, he held his father's longsword, his fingers tight about the leather grip. The blade was clean and brilliant without a drop of blood to be seen. It was as if the edges had never been used...and he felt ashamed. His long hair, damp with sea spray, hung down like a curtain to cloak him.

Nearby, a fire burned, in a hovel at the back of the beach. He wanted to lie down beside it, but something held him back. He could have closed his eyes forever, but something made him turn toward the sea, away from the heat.

The sea foamed and churned before him, as if boiling in a cauldron.

Einion stepped closer to the shore and just as both his feet entered the water, a great black wyrm rose out of it, screeching and howling, and upon its back was Gwyn ap Nudd, the Hunter, blowing his horn.

Einion dropped to his knees before the sight and sounds of horror raining down on him, and the wyrm rose to an unimaginable height, ready to drop down with gaping jaws.

No! You won't! Einion tried to roar back.

The wyrm struck downward and Einion's longsword swept up, severing the head from the body, sending the Lord of Annwn through the air to land upon his feet near the fire beyond.

Einion spun to point his sword at Gwyn ap Nudd, and the god laughed at him. *You are not mine to kill!*

He disappeared just as a great wave rushed in upon Einion, churning him with the bloody body of the wyrm, so that he struggled with all of his might to swim to the surface and cling to the rocks of the fortress above.

Einion's eyes opened with a start.

He was in a dark hovel, with stone walls that glistened with damp and firelight. The burning sensation he had been feeling had left him, his body was still now, and he felt the thick air fill his lungs again. He could not speak at first, but his eyes searched the shadows, his ears reaching out for a sound.

Then he saw her. *Gwendolyn? Alive?*

Like the sea from which he had just emerged, his memories came back to him - the moor, Lucius, Dagon, the wyrm, pain, and then her.

Gwendolyn. He allowed himself to say the name in his head, and waves of mingled love and regret washed over him. He wondered if it was another dream, but the returning feeling in his body, the pain of his leg, reminded him that he was there, in Dumnonia, and that he had come to reclaim his father's stolen throne.

Gwendolyn stood there now, resurrected.

He knew the thoughts flooding his mind distracted him from his task, from the fight ahead, but lying there, his wound burning like a divine punishment for abandoning his people, Gwendolyn, he could not help but dwell, to stare and make himself understand.

He looked up at the woman he had loved, ages ago it seemed, and he felt that seeing her, hearing her hushed voice, he was revisiting a pleasant dream from which he had been rudely awoken in another lifetime.

If she is alive, and standing there, he thought, *then surely anything is possible. If I become king in Dumnonia, then I'll ask her to be my queen... Gods, do not forsake me now.*

"He's awake," Dagon said from the other side of the fire where he and Lucius had been cleaning their armour as they spoke with Gwendolyn.

In a moment, a soft hand was gripping Einion's, and his eyes opened wide to take in the sight of Gwendolyn.

"Your fever is broken," she said, smiling, her eyes wet.

"I can't believe it's you," Einion said, his hand reaching up slowly to touch her cheek. "I thought..."

"I know," she said. "I thank the Gods that you and Briana are alive."

"More now than ever before," he said, pushing himself up slowly to sit.

They held each other with infinite tenderness then, remembering each other, and after a few moments, Lucius and Dagon approached.

"Thank the Gods, you're safe," Lucius said.

"Thought we were going to have to kill your uncle for you," Dagon said. "But I think you'll be able to do that yourself."

Einion did not answer immediately.

"Easy," Lucius said to Dagon. "He needs to rest."

"There's no time," Einion answered. "Besides, I feel fine." He tried standing but felt a wave of dizziness rush through his body, and he sat down again.

"You need a little time, " Gwendolyn said, handing him a black, clay cup of water. "You need to eat, and we need to cauterize your wound."

"That should be fun," Einion laughed weakly.

Throughout that day, many of the villagers came to Gwendolyn's door for news of the returned son of their murdered lord. They brought what food and drink they could afford to offer, as well as words of joy and comfort, of hope.

Outside, while Dagon cared for his and Einion's horses, Lucius stared out across the moor, over the rock formations, puddles, and mounds of bones the villagers had erected. The place was no longer beautiful to him, but hateful, and full of pain.

We're not here for me, he told himself. It was torturous, the thought of carrion birds, wolves and foxes tearing away at Lunaris' body while he was in that village, safe and warm. *But are we safe here?* He was not sure, still, after everything Gwendolyn had said. A part of him wanted ride out to Lunaris' corpse, and another to ride home to Adara and the children.

You do not need to go, Apollo had said. *I will not be able to help you.*

Lucius drew the sword from his back and pointed it out, toward the moor so that even the grey light gleamed upon its perfect blade. As his gaze focussed beyond the tip, he saw a group of about seven ragged-looking men coming up the muddy track toward the village.

The group seemed unbothered by the piles of bones and plagued corpses strewn about as they strode up. Lucius stepped out, ready, and saw Dagon coming over from the stable to stand with him.

They said nothing, but waited for the newcomers to speak.

One of the men, a stocky tradesman by the look of him, stepped forward to face Lucius and Dagon.

"We've come to see our returned lord," he said, his beard dripping with mist, his face splattered with mud from walking the trackway across the moor.

"No idea who you're talking about, friend," Lucius said, eyeing the cudgels and hand scythes the men carried beneath their tattered cloaks.

The man coughed and called out. "Gwendolyn!"

After a minute, Gwendolyn came out of the stone house, her hood up, to greet the men.

"They are friends," she said, turning to Lucius and Dagon. "They're here to help."

"Help is good," Dagon said. "Treachery, risky...for you."

"Don't worry lad," the older man said, extending his hand. "We've waited a long time for this."

The air was tense, and Gwendolyn could see the threat of violence in Lucius and Dagon.

"Let's all go inside before we are indeed seen by unfriendly eyes," she said, her gaze urging Lucius and Dagon to trust her.

They nodded and went inside with the rest, each of them sitting near Einion where he was propped up again before the fire, nursing the bandaged wound which had been cauterized not long before. His colour was returning, and Lucius thought he had made an incredible recovery, wondered if it was due to the task he had set for himself, and his proximity to vengeance.

The company gathered around the fire, and the men who had come greeted Einion warmly.

He was less warm toward them, but Lucius could not figure out if it was his guilt, or something in the men that made Einion hold back.

Their names were Arthrek, Cadan, Kenal, Gwalather, Clemo, Edern, and the older one who had first spoken to Lucius was Costentyn.

"How many?" Gwendolyn asked Costentyn. "How many are willing and able to come and fight for Einion?"

Lucius and Dagon looked at each other and then back to Einion who seemed, to them, not surprised by this question.

"Fifty," the older man said, twisting his beard with his thumb and thick forefinger.

"That's not many," Gwendolyn said. "But it will have to do."

"Excuse us," Lucius said, "but what is going on here?" He turned to Einion. "We need to find a way to sneak inside and take them by surprise, not lay siege to the fortress, which, from what you've told me, could withstand any siege."

"Besides, you need actual warriors to take a fortress, not -" Dagon began before being cut off.

"We can fight!" the youngest man, Arthrek, said, his hand upon a cudgel. "We're willing to die to get rid of Caradoc."

"You will be dead if you don't prepare properly," Lucius added, standing up to face Einion. "Listen, we're here to help you, Einion, but you need to trust us as you always have done. If there are extra men, we can take that into account as resources, but we need to first determine how we can get into the fortress without being noticed." Lucius turned to Gwendolyn. "Will he be recognized after all these years?"

She turned to look at Einion, and nodded slowly. "Yes. He has his father's look about him." She shook her head and stood to face Lucius across the fire. "But you must listen to me now, Dragon, for I have thought this through. We know the lay of the land here, of the fortress."

"Has my uncle changed things since being there?" Einion said, his voice bitter and full of pent-up anger.

"Yes. Now if you would just listen to me, I have an idea!" Gwendolyn burst out, her impatience with them getting the better of her.

Lucius sat back down and crossed his arms. "Forgive me," he said. "Whatever information you have will be welcome and helpful."

Gwendolyn nodded and continued. "The fortress is always well-guarded, especially on the landward side at the causeway and bridge. He has anywhere up to one-hundred and fifty men on the rock itself."

"That's why we've not considered storming it, Roman," said the one named Clemo, rubbing his bald head which shone in the firelight.

"So why do you think you can do it now?" Dagon asked.

"Because our lord has returned," said Edern from the back of the room. "The Gods have sent us a sign."

"The Gods have sent you three warriors," Lucius added. "Hardly enough to lay siege to a fortress and take on one-hundred and fifty soldiers."

"The Gods *have* sent us a sign," Gwendolyn confirmed, her hand finding Einion's shoulder. "The timing is right."

"For what, exactly?" Lucius said.

"Two days from now is the feast of Samhain," Gwendolyn said.

"So?" Dagon had his dagger in his hand and was now sharpening it. "What's that to do with a siege?"

"It's our way in," said Costentyn.

"Every year since taking the throne," Gwendolyn continued, "Caradoc has the people of these lands come to present their harvest offerings to him at the fortress. It's the only time folk are permitted to enter, to approach him in the hall, and present their gifts to him."

"It's the same night on which he stole the throne from my father," Einion said.

Lucius thought for a moment. "Go on. What's your plan?"

Gwendolyn walked around the fire, all the men's eyes on her, listening to her as if she were a bard weaving a spell of hope and daring.

"I propose, we gather our offerings as usual. We have stores of nuts, roots, and some apples. We place them in large baskets and carry them to the fortress. Inside each one, we'll hide weapons which we can draw out once we're inside."

"A moment, my lady," Dagon said. "Why would Caradoc allow anyone into the fortress if there is plague in the land? Would he risk such a thing?"

"He has men stationed on the landward side of the causeway to check people before they cross. This plague sees many sores upon the face, and blackening of the skin. Once they see that our faces are clean, they'll let us in. Caradoc allows this because he is more afraid of angering the Gods than of risking plague victims coming to the fortress. He has made it known that they would be slain on sight, tossed into the sea by his men."

There was a sad note in her voice, upon all of their faces. They had all known people who had become sick, or died of the plague.

Lucius spoke up. "You said they check people on the way in, so that makes it impossible for Einion to enter undetected. We can't guarantee that the people at the gate won't know his face."

"It's a risk, I'll grant you," Gwendolyn said.

"Risk?" Dagon said. "It's suicide! There must be another way."

"What about the sea?" Lucius added. "Do you have any ships?"

"The sea around the rock is too unforgiving for a small ship to approach, especially at a full moon," a black-haired man named Cadan said. "But there might be another way." He turned to Costentyn. "Those stairs you were ordered to carve out of the rock? What about that door?"

"There's another door?" Dagon asked.

Costentyn nodded. "Aye. When the plague hit, Caradoc ordered a stairway cut into the side of the rock facing the bay below." He turned to Einion. "You know the old tidal cave beneath the fortress?"

"I remember, yes." Einion nodded and rubbed his chin as he stared into the flames.

"Caradoc wanted to be able to go out without risking the plague beyond his gates. That was when it was at its peak. I lost a few good men carving those bloody stairs out for him, but they do lead to a postern door on the northeast edge of the fortress."

"Does it lock from the inside?" Gwendolyn asked.

Costentyn nodded.

Einion turned to Lucius and Dagon. "My friends, you're the most skilled in strategy. How would you handle this? Bearing in mind that it will be night, and we'll be greatly outnumbered."

Lucius leaned in toward the fire, the light catching the dragon upon his breast, and looked sidelong at Dagon.

"It all hangs on surprise. If everyone here and in the neighbouring villages has kept their mouths shut about Einion's return, then it could work. They can't know we're coming. If that's the case, we need as many people loyal to Einion to get in through the main gate and onto the fortress rock."

"What about us?" Einion said.

"That's where I have a plan, but it will be difficult," Gwendolyn said.

"Tell us," Einion smiled.

"While the others join the procession into the fortress, you, Lucius, and Dagon will go down to the beach beside the cave, when it is dark. You'll need to wait until the tide allows you to cross the beach. Once there, you will need to climb the stairs which Costentyn built, until you get to the postern door."

"Who will open the door?" Dagon asked.

"I will," Arthrek said, nodding his shaggy blond hair. "I can slip away from the gathering to open it."

"But it's dangerous out there, Einion," Costentyn said. "The stairs are steep, and slippery from the sea spray. One wrong move and you lads will be smashed on the rocks below."

"What if he has the beach and postern door guarded?" Lucius asked. "Those men could raise the alarm and then we'll never get in."

"Caradoc is too comfortable now. He won't suspect a thing. He thinks most of the people are too sick to oppose him," Gwendolyn said. "Besides, I can cover you with my bow from the beach."

Einion turned quickly to her. "No! You're not coming."

"Of course I am!" she said. "You need me."

"Exactly. I thought I lost you once before," Einion said. "I'm not going to lose you again."

"Listen," she gripped his hands, kneeling before him, uncaring of the others. "If you don't succeed this night, I don't want to live in this world anymore. I'm going to be there, to fight alongside you, and to see you sit on that throne. Else, I'll die beside you in battle."

"You almost sound Sarmatian," Dagon said, smiling, thinking of Briana then.

Lucius was silent, considering what Gwendolyn said. "She's right, Einion. We could use her bow...if she's any good with it." Lucius looked at her and she smiled slyly. "Are you?"

"I can pluck a hare off its feet at a hundred paces," she said proudly.

"Standing still, though," Dagon added.

"Running," she replied.

"That will work," Lucius laughed. "Once Arthrek opens the door, you can provide covering fire from the shadows." He looked at Einion. "You have your strategy, my friend."

"What happens once we're inside?" Dagon said.

"The hall is large. That's where Caradoc will be sitting," Gwendolyn said. "It will be crowded with people, and offerings. Bonfires will be burning all over the fortress, and in the centre of the hall."

"It'll be chaotic once we attack," Lucius said, turning to the seven men before him. "If you and your people can slay as many of Caradoc's troops as possible before being discovered, that will help. We can cut our way to Caradoc and then," he turned to Einion, "you'll have your chance to face him."

"Are my uncle's men utterly loyal to him?" Einion asked Gwendolyn.

"I don't know," she said. "Maybe, for he keeps them clothed, and fed, and drunk, when the rest of Dumnonia is starving, and Rome turns a blind eye."

Lucius felt a tinge of guilt then. In the past he was naive enough to think that Rome would have cared for the lives of the people in the territories it conquered, but that was not the case in Dumnonia.

"And yet," Dagon said, "when the head of the snake is cut off, the rest of the body becomes useless and flailing." Dagon noticed Lucius stare into the flames then, and put a hand upon his shoulder. "We're with you, Einion."

Lucius stood and nodded. "To the death."

Einion stood then and faced all of them, his longsword held tightly in his fist as he looked each man in the face.

"I know I have not been here for all of you for years, and that you have suffered. I also know you risk much to fight for me now, that the odds are against us."

"We are with you, Einion, son of Cunnomore," Costentyn said, standing before the others. "If the Roman Dragon can fight to the death for his friend, so can we for our rightful lord...our king!"

The men echoed the words and there was indeed fire and belief in their world-weary eyes.

Einion felt a thrill run through his body and he stood even taller then, the pain in his leg a distant memory in the face of the people before him, his people.

"I will kill Caradoc, I swear to you!" he said, his voice intense. "But if I do not, then I will die such a death that my father will finally cry my name from the far shores of Annwn."

The men yelled, for they could not help it, experiencing that feeling one gets when life and strength return after a long illness.

97

Behind Einion and Gwendolyn, Lucius and Dagon smiled at each other and nodded as Einion spoke.

"My brothers, by Samhain night, we shall be back in my father's hall!"

VII

SANGUINIS OBLATIO

'Blood Offerings'

They gathered at the village the following day, people with carts and baskets, emerging from the cracks and crevices of the moor and its tors to come join Einion and march on his ancestral fortress.

Lucius and Dagon watched them come and bow to Einion, a man most had barely remembered except through here-say and rumour.

"This feels strange, doesn't it?" Dagon said to Lucius.

"How so?" Lucius said, reaching up to feel the handle of his sword at his back.

"We're used to riding to battle, headlong into the enemy, or waiting for him to jump out. But now," Dagon shook his head, "we seem to be going in like thieves and assassins."

"For our friends," Lucius said.

"Yes. I think this is the first time I've not fought a battle for Rome," Dagon said. "I was too young when my people fought the Romans. I've always fought for them. And now... I suppose this is just different," Dagon shrugged.

"This time, it feels right," Lucius said. "Except I won't be riding to battle."

Dagon nodded and leaned on the stone wall that looked out to the moor. "I've seen some things in my time with you, Lucius Metellus Anguis, but never did I think we would have seen a monster like that."

"And I have a feeling it's not over..." Lucius mumbled, before walking away.

Dagon watched him go out onto the moor, past the gathered villagers, each of whom was checking crude weapons and tucking them carefully into their offering baskets and sacks - butcher's blades, hand scythes, rusty daggers, and sacrificial blades that had not seen offerings for a long while.

"Will he be all right?" Einion asked, leaning against the wall beside Dagon.

"Yes," Dagon answered immediately. "Anguis has never let us down. He just needs time alone. The Gods will rally him as they always do." Dagon turned to Einion. "So, Lord Einion... When do we leave?"

"Close to dusk. We must travel all night and part of the next day to arrive at the fortress by dusk at Samhain."

"We'll be exposed on the road."

"I know the ways still, as does Gwendolyn," Einion said confidently. "We'll be shielded from unfriendly eyes."

"I hope so, my friend," Dagon said. "Else your throne may elude you."

Einion was silent a moment. "That's not an option," he finally said.

The procession of fifty set off northwest across the moor once the sun lay upon the horizon. Every man and woman went forth in the torn and tattered rags of the plague people, but now relieved of the theatre of their sickness. Many of the people felt strange walking out of doors, not trying to appear sick. However, their fear was plain enough upon their faces, for most had never dared approach the fortress since Caradoc had taken the throne.

Dagon watched them all as he walked, leading his horse with bundles upon its back, some food, rope and hooks should they be needed to scale the rock walls of the fortress. He wondered if the villagers would have the courage to rise up when the time came. As a king himself, he knew Einion would have to lead by example in the fight. The people would follow, and fight, but only if their lord did so. Dagon then looked across the back of his horse at Lucius who walked with the black hood of his cloak up, shielding his face from everyone.

Lucius had been quiet since the wyrm was slain, since Lunaris had died... *As fine a death as any warrior's,* Dagon thought. *Lucius...snap out of it, my friend.*

Lucius looked toward him as if he had heard his thoughts, and Dagon nodded. There were no words at this point. The time for fighting was nearing, and each of them dealt with the thoughts and wishes pressing upon their minds, the prayers whispered to the Gods under hushed breaths.

Lucius, for his part, felt strange not leading his cavalry to battle. This time, standing beside peasants, the objective was to put Einion, their lord, back upon his throne. *We have that in common at least,* he thought.

Ahead, Einion and Gwendolyn walked at a steady pace, leading one of the wagons laden with baskets of offerings.

Lucius thought that Einion stood taller, seemed stronger with every league they travelled over the green and muddy moor, passing in the shadows of the tors, and following the gently sloping land toward the sea.

The land appeared to change about them too. The rains had retreated and the moon emerged from behind the departing clouds to reveal a titanic orb, one day short of its fullness, yellow and cold where it hung in the sky.

As the procession of the would-be lord of Dumnonia passed, it was as if some memory that had lain fallow in the land began to course with life. That is, until full darkness fell, and the shadows clawed at them.

They marched all night beneath the yellow light, armies of black clouds ripping across the moon's face, making their passage difficult.

"Are we going the right way?" Lucius asked Einion as he walked beside him and Dagon at the front now, while Gwendolyn hung back with the women, Caja, Ebrel, and Melwyn.

"Yes, but the light is making it tough. If one of the wagons goes off the side of one of the higher roads, then we're lost."

"What's that noise?" Dagon suddenly said in the darkness, his sword sliding out.

"Hold!" Einion whispered into the darkness behind them. They stood still, trying to hear beyond the scared breathing of the villagers behind them.

Lucius felt a dread in the pit of his stomach and closed his eyes for a moment. "It's a hunting horn," he said.

"Gods help us," Costentyn said behind them. "Gwynn ap Nudd is abroad this night."

There were rumblings of dread all around, and it was all Lucius could do to shut out the increasingly loud call of the horn upon the black moors.

"We have to keep going," Einion said. "Forward!" he hissed.

The train continued on its way, but every person there now bore a burden of dread, for the Wild Hunt was but a day away, and the lord of Annwn was already riding upon the moor around them.

Leave them alone, Lucius thought as he remembered facing the tall dark figure days before, and the terrified face of the nymph whom the Lord of Annwn had hunted.

When the ghostly horn ceased to call out in the night, Lucius could still hear it in his mind, could still feel the land wanting to swallow him up, the rocks to crush him, and every tree want to rip into him.

When dawn came, they were proceeding down a sunken road hedged in on both sides, well-shielded from enemy eyes. Some of the villagers looked around in awe at the changes wrought over the previous night upon the moor, the downs, and the river streams. The changes were unnoticed at first. The leaves of the few scattered trees upon the moor, or ranked alongside streams, grew more golden in their autumnal transit, green shoots emerged from the muddy earth as if to watch the world again, braver now, more daring than they had been in the span of their young lives.

And with the wyrm slain by their rightful lord and his friends, animals who had burrowed deep into the earth now came out into the light of day. Something was happening, the walking villagers said, but none would dare utter the thoughts coming to mind.

By dusk the next day, they came to a stone bridge that arched over a low-flowing river, set deep into the ground like a brown vein in the landscape, or a sword gash from a titan's weapon. The company pulled off the road and hid in a thick copse of trees to allow darkness to fall.

Only the wind was to be heard above the sound of trickling water at the bottom of the steep slope above the river. Several ravens cawed in the trees above them, as if waiting for the night, watching.

Lucius looked up at them and wondered if Apollo, Venus, and Epona were indeed watching him, or if they truly could not see him in that land.

Guide my hand this night...if you can hear me...

Lucius felt a strong grip on his shoulder and turned to see Dagon, concern in his eyes as he looked at him.

"Anguis," he whispered. "You ready for this?"

Lucius looked at him and nodded. "Yes," he said, automatically.

Beside them, Gwendolyn and Einion were going over the plan one more time with Costentyn and the others. When they had done, and darkness began to cover the world, they watched the procession get onto the road to the fortress, a couple of leagues away.

"Now it's up to us," Einion said, turning to the three of them.

"Samhain is upon us, and the fires will be blazing soon," Gwendolyn said. "We should move now." She slung a thick quiver of arrows over her shoulder and gripped a small recurve bow in her left hand.

"We're with you, Einion," Dagon said.

Lucius stepped up to his friend and put his hands upon his shoulders. "We'll cut a path to Caradoc for you, no matter what. I swear that you will sit upon your throne by the end of this night."

As if in angry retort, the hunting horn blasted louder than ever before in the distance, and the four of them fought the shivers that laced up and down their backs.

"Let's go," Einion said, hefting his sword and quitting the shelter of the trees for the narrow path in the direction of the sea.

As they jogged along, with the two horses trailing behind them, a full moon erupted from behind a thick bank of clouds. Red light infused the world about them, as if in warning.

"It's a blood moon," Gwendolyn said, her voice shaken, despite her brave attitude. "Gods help us this night."

To Lucius and Dagon, the night would be one to haunt memory, not for the coming fight, but for the strange goings on all around them. Beyond the dismal call of that hunting horn, there was a constant wailing on the wind as of tortured shades come into the world of men to harangue the living.

Loud crashes could be heard upon the moor, and in the sky. Screams to chill the blood assaulted man, woman and child.

At one point, Lucius stopped running and drew his sword, the blade pointed at the sky above where he spied winged shadows soaring across the face of the moon.

"What are those?" he said, trying to be heard above the wind and sound of screaming.

"There's another one!" Dagon yelled, his own sword raised in one hand while his other held on tightly to the reins of his increasingly spooked horse.

"Banshees!" Gwendolyn said, pulling at them to keep following Einion who had continued on ahead. "Quickly, we must keep going!"

The wind picked up, as if it were trying to drown out the raucous sounds of the night, and they pressed on, down black slopes and across bald patches of land until the sea stretched out before them, black, and deep, a storm-tossed abyss awaiting with open arms.

Einion stopped and waited, his gaze straying to the East, a short distance down the coastline, where it seemed great fires blazed upon a giant, black rock. He felt Gwendolyn grip his arm, and he turned to her, Lucius and Dagon. Without saying anything, for fear of his voice being carried on the wind, he pointed.

They all stared at it for a few moments, untwisting their wind-whipped cloaks, checking their weapons, and calming the two horses.

With a nod, Einion led the way along the cliffs, a meandering route, in and out along the edges, the fortress rock ever before them, getting larger, and brighter with every step they took in that red, howling night.

When they were close enough to see smaller, individual fires dotting the headland of the fortress, Einion held up his hand and crouched behind a line of weathered stone where a small lean-to had been constructed to shelter grazing sheep in days gone by.

"We need to leave the horses here," Einion said, tying up his mount. "The fortress bay is just below us now. We need to scale our way down."

"Show me," Lucius said to Gwendolyn as Dagon began hitching his own horse.

Gwendolyn nodded and crouched, edging around the rockface with Lucius and then crawling upon her stomach to the cliff's edge.

"This is where we climb down," she said.

Lucius looked over the edge and all he could see were varying shades of blackness, leading to a great fire upon the beach where six men stood. In the bay, two ships sat at anchor, their bodies rolling up and down on the breakers as the tide rushed in. Apart from the rush of the wind, Lucius could hear the raging seas as if he were alone upon a branch in a Middle Sea storm.

Breathe, Lucius... he told himself. *Breathe.*

"The tide is coming in," Gwendolyn said. "We must get down there now." She turned around and went back to Einion and Dagon while Lucius stared down at the beach and then up at the fortress.

The rock was massive, shear and terrifying. The waves crashed upon it and spray shot high into the air to be infused with red moonlight like sprays of blood in the arena at night. The rock reminded Lucius of a great kraken of Neptune's, a beast crawling out of the sea to ravage the green lands beyond.

And now, we have to climb it...

He went back to join the others. "I hope Costentyn is right about the stairs in the rock," Lucius said when he was beneath the lean-to "I can't see anything of the sort."

"You won't at night," Einion said.

"Just follow me, and step where I step," Gwendolyn said. "The stairs are small, but they'll be there."

"But first we need to climb down," Einion sheathed his sword and felt the two daggers at his waist. "Ready?"

"Ready," Lucius and Dagon said in concert, each having checked their own weapons.

They crawled along to the cliff's edge and waited to see if the men on the beach spotted them in the red light.

The six figures stood close to their protective bonfire, passing around an amphora of wine, blind to the darkness beyond.

"Let's go!" Gwendolyn hissed as she began the descent.

Einion, Lucius and Dagon followed her.

There was a line of suppliants waiting in the darkness upon the road, to cross the bridge to the fortress. Most had come in small groups, each holding baskets of browning apples, nuts, black bread, or fleeces.

Costentyn, Arthrek and the others behind them peered ahead to where a large group of guards poked into people's baskets, and shone their torches on their terrified faces to ensure there were no sores upon them.

"They're checking the baskets," Arthrek whispered to Costentyn.

"Keep your voice down," the older man said, turning to look back at the long line of their people. "Kenal, Ewella, make sure all the horses are tied up securely. We can't take them across. Everybody else, take a basket of offerings to bring to Lord Caradoc!"

The villagers complied and began hefting baskets and bags, while Kenal and Ewella, tied up the wagon and horses on the side of the road with several others before rejoining the group.

All of them were nervous, the rank sweat of their fear easily detected. But it was not only the soldiers a few feet away that bothered them - the shrill cries from those unseen in the sky were ten times more fearful, and many wished they had not come.

"Plague!" one of the guards suddenly yelled farther up the line.

Suddenly, several people were screaming, and a lone couple at the front were isolated at spear point.

"Get out of here!" another guard yelled.

"We have nowhere to go, lord," a frail, old man's voice said. "We are sure our lord can heal us if we but give him our offerings!"

"Fools," Costentyn muttered.

"Shall we help?" Arthrek asked.

"No. Lord Einion is depending on us."

There was a scream from the old woman as a spear point pricked her side, and the troops pushed them away. But they persisted in trying to gain the bridge until the guard gave the order to his men.

"Over the side with'em then!"

Four guards moved in with their spears levelled and prodded the old couple like aged cattle, too tired to comply. There was a last scream and then silence as they tumbled over the cliff's edge to the rocks far below.

The guards stared into the blackness for a moment, and then returned to their posts.

"Next!" the head guard called out, and the line moved forward.

"Bastards!" the woman Caja said behind Arthrek.

"Keep it down," Costentyn said. "We just need to get through. Stay in line, show them the baskets and your faces and move on."

The group moved forward and they could see the bridge dipping away over the blackness, from the causeway to the fortress.

Beyond, the expanse of the rock itself seemed to seethe with Samhain bonfires. The heat from two great fires behind the guards could be felt now. The fortress' threshold had to be purified with the sacred fire, as did all who passed through that in-between place.

Costentyn and the others could see the bonfires upon the rock where they were surrounded by the ghostly shadows of more of Caradoc's troops and those from neighbouring villages who had been forced to come and give offerings to their underserving lord.

The shapes shuddered beneath fluttering cloaks in the sharp-toothed wind, and some of the villagers thought that they might be the banshees they had heard in the dark on their journey, come down to gorge themselves on those forced to remain out of the lord's hall after they had made their offerings.

"Courage, my friends," Costentyn said as he hefted a basket and led the way to the fires before the bridge and the sharpened points of the guards' spears.

The wind howled and the rope bridge swayed, making the person crossing it at that moment drop his basket and curse into the darkness.

"Pull back your hoods!" the guard said to Costentyn and the others behind him.

They did so and allowed the soldiers to hold their torches close to their faces, and search them for weapons. It took some time for them to look at all of them, but they returned and nodded to their commander.

"What have you brought for Lord Caradoc?" the guard said, as he looked into Costentyn's basket and swept his dagger blade in among the hazelnuts.

"Nuts and the best of our apple harvests upon the moors," Costentyn said. "Also many fleeces of black and white from those herds the wyrm has not slaughtered."

The guard stopped and stared at Costentyn, and then Arthrek, as the rest of his men went down the line, poking the nuts and fleeces, or touching the apples upon the surface.

Arthrek tensed, waited for a scream or scuffle from farther down the line, and Costentyn nudged him.

"What's wrong with you?" the guard demanded of the younger man.

Arthrek made to speak but Costentyn jumped in. "None of us want to be out on a night such as this. You've heard the banshees in the skies above, haven't you? And the blaring horns of the wild huntsmen?

"Peasants!" the guard spat. "No backbone, eh? Our fires burn bright and high. Our lord has no need to fear the shades of the dead on Samhain's eve, for he has his own allies."

"Then let us give him our offerings and depart," Costentyn said. "For our fires do not burn so brightly as those upon the fortress rock."

The guard was silent a moment and then waved his hand to the entire group. "Move along!"

They began to file past and proceeded to cross the bridge. "Take your offerings directly to the fortress hall at the top of the road. You may then stay without until morning, if that is your wish, or take your chances upon the moor with the wyrm and huntsmen upon your heals!" he laughed, the sound echoed by the other soldiers.

The villagers moved on.

The walk across the bridge was not easy with the heavy baskets, and it swayed above the abyss like a flimsy washing line between two oaks in a gale.

At one point Edern stumbled and three apples from his basket tumbled over the side, but he regained his footing and pressed on, bringing up the rear.

"This way! Pass between the fires!" another guard ordered.

Costentyn led the way, a silent prayer to his gods upon his heart as he went along the road that wound up along the eastern side of the fortress rock.

Eyes peered at them from the various fires where some ate and drank, huddled together, while younger women peeled apples and flung the spirals over their shoulders and into the flames. Every twenty feet, guards stood at the ready, some drinking, others silent and staring.

When they reached the point where the road turned to go up to the fortress plateau, Arthrek broke away into the shadows.

He pressed himself into the hollow of a broken wall and watched the rest of his people pass along on the winding path to the top. He held his breath when a group of three soldiers marched along behind the group, and waited until they had passed as well before he put his basket down among some building rubble, hidden from prying eyes.

Along the outer wall...and then down a short flight of stairs... he tried to remember what Costentyn had told him, breathing deeply to calm his nerves. He knew he had to get a move-on, as Lord Einion and his friends were counting on him. The success of the mission rested on him getting that door open.

Arthrek, knelt before the basket and tipped some of the nuts out onto the grass until the hilt of a rusty gladius came into view. Luckily, the howling of the wind covered the noise he made, but he was no less wary, for the fortress was crawling with Caradoc's troops.

With the dull blade in his hand, Arthrek crept along the outer wall, twice stumbling in the dark for the uneven ground beneath his feet. He paused when the wall concealing him ended and he spied the stairs going down.

That must be it! He wiped the sweat from his brow and peeked around the corner. There, he saw the figure of a lone guard standing where the roadway veered off to the stairs to the outer door to the harbour.

The man was warming himself by a brazier in the wind and drinking from a leather wine sack.

Arthrek was about to creep past when the man turned.

"Oi! You! What are you doing there?" He began to walk toward Arthrek who had turned his back to the guard without saying anything. "I'm talking to you!" the guard said.

As soon as Arthrek felt the man's hand grab his shoulder, he turned and plunged the rusty blade of his aged gladius into the man's guts.

The man clawed at his face, but Arthrek twisted the blade and the man weakened, allowing Arthrek to drag him into the shadows.

Arthrek dropped at the sound of more people and paused to watch a group of villagers walking slowly up the hill with their baskets and firebrands. When they had passed, Arthrek moved to the top of the stairs and looked down to see a small stone landing where another brazier burned brightly.

Two more men stood around it, warming their hands, seemingly wishing they were indoors rather than out.

Arthrek stepped back, pulled the cloak of his hood over his head, and wrapped himself in the dark wool before descending the stairs toward the guards.

Sea spray lashed Einion, Lucius, Dagon, and Gwendolyn's faces as they watched the group of Caradoc's men from behind the rocks on the far side of the beach.

The climb down had been treacherous, and three times one of them had almost fallen into the teeth of the sea far below. They wanted to wait for a moment when they reached the bottom, but Gwendolyn pushed them on.

"The tide is coming in and soon we won't be able to get across to the stairs," she said as loud as she could dare.

"We need to take them by surprise," Lucius said, scanning the beach. "Maybe Dagon and I can sneak around behind them?"

Dagon peered over the rocks to see the jagged formations hidden in darkness beyond the light of the guards' fire. "If we go in low and quiet, we should be able to do it," he confirmed.

"All right," Einion said. "You approach them from behind - ask them something - and once they turn toward you, Gwendolyn and I will attack from this side."

"With my bow, I should be able to take at least two of them out before they know what's happening," Gwendolyn said.

Lucius and Dagon nodded, drew their swords and crept away in the darkness with the sound of crashing waves masking their footfalls upon the shingle and sand.

Gwendolyn turned to Einion then.

"Promise me something," she said in his ear.

He turned to her, his hair plastered against his face. "What?"

"That if we live through this, we will never be apart again." Her hand reached up and touched his cheek, and he grabbed it and kissed her.

"I can promise more than that," he said, smiling broadly.

Just then, they heard voices farther down the beach.

"Get your arrows ready," Einion said, drawing his longsword and standing up in the gathering water of the tide, ready to run.

"Excuse me?" Lucius said as he and Dagon emerged from behind the rocks at the back of the beach. Their cloaks were wrapped tightly to hide their weapons, but the men were wary and drew their own.

"What are you doing here?" a man with black armour to match that of three others said. Evidently, he was one of Caradoc's men. "No one's allowed down here, stranger. I suggest you go back to the fortress entrance to give your offerings." He scanned Lucius and Dagon and saw that they had nothing to offer. "If you're just here to whore and take Lord Caradoc's food, then this'll be your last night."

"Easy, friend," Lucius said. "It's a cold, harrowing night to be out of doors, and the tide is coming in." He nodded to where the waves were lapping at the edges of their bonfire. "We were out on the moor and heard strange goings on."

"What superstitious people you have here!" laughed one of the ship captains on the other side of the fire.

Lucius could tell right away the man was Greek, and spoke to him in his own tongue. "I suggest you go back to your ship before you die."

"What did you say?" the captain asked.

Out of the darkness a black arrow tore into the neck of one of the guards so that he crashed into the flames of the fire sending sparks into the sky.

Lucius and Dagon's blades swept up from beneath their cloaks in a second and two more of the men fell down, while the other two leapt at them. Steel clanged on the beach as the bonfire sputtered and died in the rapidly rising waters.

Dagon spun and slashed his foe across the neck so that he fell grasping into the bloody sea foam.

Lucius began to run after the other man, but Einion was already on his way and sliced so viciously at him out of the darkness that his head came clean off.

"Where's the ship captain?" Lucius said.

They searched around and spotted a man running clumsily up the rock staircase at the far side of the beach.

"Hurry! He'll alert the others!" Einion cried, running after the man, followed by Gwendolyn, Lucius, and Dagon.

They felt around for the stairs, their eyes straining in the red moonlight, searching for the beginning of the steps.

"Here they are!" Einion said, going up as quickly as he could, only to see that the captain was already at the door.

As the captain pulled back his arm to pound, he froze and pitched backward over the cliff's edge to crash into the churning water far below.

At the twang of the bowstring, Lucius turned to see Gwendolyn straightening up at the bottom of the stairs and walking toward him.

"Nice shot," he said.

"I have my moments, Dragon," she answered.

They climbed more carefully after that, the rocks slippery and dark beneath their feet, causing them to slip often.

At one point, Lucius looked down to the blackness below where the sea roared mightily, and he thought that one wrong move would be the end of him.

Gods, guide us on our way...

When they all reached the top, perched precariously on the side of the steep-sloped cliff, they drew their swords again.

Einion put his ear to the door and heard scuffling on the other side, a desperate panting, choking, and then a muffled cry of pain.

Gwendolyn looked up at him, fear in her eyes. "He's been killed," she whispered. "We'll never get in now."

Einion's heart sank, but he steeled himself for the worst and nodded to the others before knocking six times as they had agreed. If it was Arthrek, he would open, if it was the guards, then they would have to fight through, or be pushed into the sea below.

For a moment, nothing happened. In the light of the fire on the other side, creeping beneath the door, blood ran like honey about their feet where they were about to enter the fortress.

"Open up!" Einion yelled.

A bolt slid on the other side, and the door opened slowly to reveal Arthrek, his face bloodied, his nose broken, but the bodies of both guards lying on the ground at his feet, soaking the stone landing.

Gwendolyn looked him over. "Are you badly injured?"

Arthrek shook his head, his hand going to stop the blood running from his nose.

Einion stepped forward and pat the younger man on the shoulder. "Good lad," he said, bringing a smile to Arthrek's face. "You've done well."

"We need to douse this fire," Dagon said, pointing at the brazier. "We can't clean this mess up. We just have to hope no one notices it before we're done."

Lucius was already picking up one of the guard's helmets and dipping it into a nearby rain bucket to scoop the water out. Soon the fire was hissing and the bodies were covered in shadow.

"Which way to the hall?" Lucius asked Einion.

The latter looked at Gwendolyn and nodded. "The way we used to walk? The outer path to the top?"

She nodded. "Yes. That way we can get there with fewer people seeing us. Everyone put your hoods up and sheathe your swords for now. If anyone sees us, we've already made our offerings."

They all did as she suggested, and followed Einion up a narrow path that wound round to the north side of the rock, facing the sea.

The fortress was vast and dark the way they went, and the wind more violent once they curved around the northern, sea-facing side of the fortress. What fires had been lit there were no longer burning, but cold and grey.

Finally, they turned left up a small path that led directly to the top of the fortress.

"Wait!" Einion put out his hand and stopped the others. "Guards."

They looked around the end of a low wall to see four guards gathered there.

"Better to kill them now than to have to deal with them and a load of others later," Lucius said. "Can you take out the one on the right with your bow?" he asked Gwendolyn.

She looked and nodded.

"You watch her back while we take care of the others," Einion said to Arthrek.

They wrapped their cloaks about themselves again and strolled out and up the path.

Immediately, the guards looked their way, their swords pointed at them.

"Stop there!" one of them ordered, but the three men kept moving toward them.

Without waiting for an answer, the guard in front swung his sword at Dagon.

The latter sidestepped it and plunged a dagger into his gut, even as Lucius and Einion launched themselves forward at the other two, ducking under the reach of their swords and running their own daggers to the hilt in their guts or throats.

The fourth man fell upon their bodies with an arrow in his back, completing the number.

Einion motioned for them to follow him quickly and, like thieves in the night, they scurried through the shadows, hearts racing, to reach the plateau of the fortress where they emerged into a world of orange flame.

Bonfires burned everywhere, all radiating from a central larger one where several guards were gathered.

Einion led the way around the fire, gazing at the huddled forms of people trying to stay warm, eating scraps tossed to them by Caradoc. They shuddered at the unearthly noises on the wind and out upon the moor. It pained his heart to see such things, but he pressed on, the roofline of the stone hall coming into view in the orange and red light cast by fires and the moon. At one of the outer fires, he heard a cry as two girls were being accosted by drunk guards, ignored by those all about them as they tore at the girls' clothing.

Gwendolyn reached for his arm to pull him toward the hall, but Einion was already on his way to the fire, walking quickly, determinedly, his blade no longer hidden.

"Wait your turn!" one of the guards said without really seeing Einion approach, and as he was about to thrust into the girl, Einion had him by the hair and was stabbing him in the throat, tossing the body into the darkness.

The other man stumbled to his feet from the girl he was with, but before he could reach for his blade, Einion had run him through.

"Go! Get out of here," he said to the two girls who looked up, gape-mouthed and shuddering. He looked at them more calmly now. "It will all be well. Go. Hide until morning."

The girls disappeared into the shadows as Einion returned to the others.

"That was risky," Lucius said. "Good thing those guards over there are even more drunk than these two."

"I'm not leaving till every one of them is dead," Einion said.

"We'll help you, my friend," Lucius said.

"But first, you have a snake to kill," Dagon added. "Is that the hall?"

"Yes. They'll be in there." Einion wiped the sweat from his brow and pulled his hood up again. His fingers were beginning to shake, but he fought back the nerves. *The Gods won't abandon me now,* he hoped.

"I can't see Costentyn and the others," Gwendolyn said, her eyes searching the darkness between fires.

"There they are!" Arthrek pointed with a bloody hand. "Near the third fire from the doors to the hall."

They began to move that way, toward the group. Some people stared at them as they passed, but most ignored them, content to huddle beneath their cloaks and avoid the gaze of any of the troops dotting the area.

When they were within sight of Costentyn's group, Einion nodded to the older man and they began to gather their baskets and crowd into the hall entrance where bright braziers burned and guards stared everyone in the face.

"You need to stay outside," Einion said to Arthrek. "If they see your face covered in blood, they'll suspect something's happened. Stay near the side door and watch for other guards running in. Can you do that?"

"You can count on me, my lord," Arthrek said.

Einion paused, only now just realizing that the young man before him would follow him, that he did indeed view him as their lord, as did all of the villagers waiting to fight by his side. They looked to him, and waited for him to enter the hall that was rightfully his.

Einion, Lucius and the others picked up baskets that were brought by the others of their group, and lined up to flow into the hall.

As they approached, Einion looked up at the low, wind-battered roof, remembered how many times he had walked through that doorway for celebrations with his family, and his people. Now, he was going in to avenge the wrong done to all of them, an event that had torn his and Briana's lives to bloody pieces. He gripped the basket of apples tightly, but was keenly aware of the sword and daggers hidden beneath his cloak as he went.

Lucius and Dagon followed behind him, side by side in the battle line as ever, and Gwendolyn and the rest of the villagers crowded in behind.

"Slowly now!" one of the guards yelled, trying to look at everyone's faces as they entered the fortress hall.

Einion's eyes adjusted to the light inside, and he cast his gaze around the realm of his lost youth. As he waited to step forward to present his basket, he felt anger surge at the changes wrought by Caradoc.

There had been a time when the stone walls of his father's hall were alight with golden fire, warm and welcoming, where wine had filled guests' cups to brimming, and the people's faces had shone with a rosy hue like that of a bright clear dawn in Spring.

But now, soldiers lined the walls of the hall instead of garlands and casks, the sharpened weaponry upon the walls echoing the menace of the people's host.

Einion remembered being at odds with his father, often, but he knew that the people would have been welcomed as guests by their lord. Now, however, they cowered like beasts, with white-faced fear, hunched and starving and dressed in rags as they handed over great portions of their winter stores to the tyrant lord of Dumnonia.

Einion pressed farther into the crowd. He could feel Lucius and Dagon at his back, and see Costentyn and others fanning out in the densely-packed hall. He could not yet see his uncle for all the people and the hovering smoke from the hearth, but he knew he was there, his arrogant voice barking a word now and then, but never uttering a word of thanks to those he perceived as lower than himself.

The smoke wafted as people moved around, and Einion got closer.

Finally, Caradoc came into view and Einion stopped abruptly, feeling Lucius' hand upon his shoulder.

Caradoc sat upon the stone throne, his gaze as cold as iron, matching the blade of black steel that lay across his lap. He was more grey than he had once been, but no less of a bear in size and strength.

As people came before him, silent and solemn, to lay their baskets and offerings between the burning braziers at his feet, he stared at them as if they were bugs to be crushed beneath his boot.

Meanwhile, his advisors behind him laughed and joked and drank like the guards around the fires dotting the fortress rock beneath the blood moon.

Behind Einion, Lucius and Dagon searched the crowd for Caradoc's soldiers.

"You see them?" Lucius asked.

"Oh, yes. About twenty, I'd say, plus those outside. Could be double," Dagon sighed. For a moment, he thought of Briana, and how he was there for her as much as for Einion.

"I'll go left, you go right," Lucius whispered. He squeezed Einion's shoulder again. "You ready?"

Einion's head turned slightly, but just then, he seemed stunned, his eyes staring beyond the throne.

Lucius and Dagon could not tell what he saw.

Could Einion have spoken then, he would have, but the weeping shades of his parents behind Caradoc caused him to hesitate. *Mother? Father?* Einion thought, and he could see them staring at him. His mother wept and clutched at the ghostly gash in her neck. His father, bleeding from countless wounds to his body simply stared at Einion then, and at his brother, with eyes full of hate and vengeance.

Lucius saw Einion nod, and heard him mutter something beneath his breath. "You all right?" he hissed. They could see the eyes of the villagers who had followed them staring their way, and Lucius worried that they would draw attention to Einion.

Dagon and Lucius put down their baskets and gripped their swords beneath their cloaks.

"Step forward with your offerings, peasants! Lord Caradoc does not have all night to wait upon you!" said a plump man beside Einion's uncle.

In that moment, Einion snapped out of his reverie, and forced himself to ignore the shades flanking the throne.

An old woman came forward with a small bundle of nuts which she had gathered in a tattered rag, and bent painfully before Caradoc.

"What is this?" Caradoc growled.

"My offering to you, lord Caradoc, on this sacred night of Samhain," she croaked, as she unwrapped the bundle with her gnarled fingers. "Please accept my humble offering."

The advisor beside Caradoc descended the steps and, with a sneer, kicked the woman so that she squealed as she fell over on her side upon the stone floor.

"My lord Caradoc!" Einion's voice suddenly filled the hall and all fell silent. "Is this how you honour your people before the Gods on this sacred night?"

All eyes turned toward the three cloaked figures in the centre of the hall.

Einion walked forward to help the old woman to her feet as she crawled away from the throne toward him. Bending over, he held her thin frame in his hands and lifted her to her feet.

With cloudy eyes, she studied Einion and put her bony hand to his cheek.

"Do not worry," he told her.

She nodded, and a light seemed to come into her eyes as she made her way back into the crowd.

"How dare you speak like that to his lordship in his own hall!" the advisor said. "Guards!"

There was movement along the walls, in front and behind them.

Einion removed his hood at stared at Caradoc.

"Do you remember me, Uncle?"

For a moment, Caradoc's face was utterly disbelieving, but he rallied himself quickly. His eyes narrowed, and he held up his hand for the guards to stop moving in.

The hall was laced with panic, as the world is before the first crack of lighting in a storm. There was nowhere for people to move, and so they stared, many unable to comprehend what was happening.

Caradoc laughed.

"So, you're not dead, Nephew. Quite grown up, in fact." Caradoc looked Einion over as if in approval of his form, though not standing from the throne. "What is it you want? Do you bring me a basket of apples?"

"You are undeserving of these sacred offerings," Einion said slowly, indicating the baskets and bundles upon the floor. "You have no right to sit there!" He pointed at the throne.

Caradoc laughed again.

"I have every right to sit here. I am the strongest in these lands." Now Caradoc stood. "And I killed your father right here." He pointed at the ground where the offerings now stood.

"That throne is not yours," Einion said. "This is not your kingdom!"

"If you want it," Caradoc said, "you will have to kill *me* for it."

Einion drew his father's sword and pointed it at his uncle.

"Tonight, I'll offer your blood to the Gods, Uncle."

There was a momentary pause in which only the flickering of the hearth flames could be heard, and then people were screaming.

Einion, Lucius and Dagon were swallowed up in a fast moving wave of guards.

"Kill them!" Caradoc bellowed, as an arrow plunged into the neck of his fat advisor whose body folded down the steps to catch in the fire.

The world moved slowly in the eye of the storm in which Einion, Lucius and Dagon fought, for the three warriors, after being pushed back, now cut into their foes with vigour.

Einion leapt in first, with Lucius and Dagon at his flanks. They cut and slashed, and stabbed at Caradoc's men like three lions wading into a pack of hyenas.

Despite the bite of enemy blades, the three warriors attacked, pushed back, and slew the enemy without mercy.

The paving slabs were thick with blood and littered with corpses. The bodies of writhing men grabbed and stabbed at Einion, Lucius, and Dagon's feet, but the villagers had now found their courage and were dispatching the downed enemies, loosing their pent-up rage upon Caradoc's men.

Einion moved in a trance, every thrust finding a home, every cut a limb, so that the bodies built up before him, and the blood coated his person.

To the left and right, Lucius and Dagon mauled the enemy, giving Einion the room he needed to cut his way toward his target.

"Lucius!" Dagon yelled. "The door!"

Lucius turned to see more men pouring in from the side door toward them, but at that moment, the tide was slowed as they saw Arthrek hacking them from behind, and Clemo and Kenal from inside the hall.

Lucius then saw Dagon go down and rushed over to his side, but the Sarmatian king cried with fury and the men who had piled upon him, stabbing at his armoured body, were suddenly flung off like a horse swats at errant flies.

Lucius turned to see the villagers fighting desperately with the guards at the entrance to the hall. Above, like cicadas buzzing across a summer field, Gwendolyn's arrows passed and plucked the life out of black-uniformed men, weakening the line before Caradoc. Lucius turned back to fight by Einion's side. He did not hear Gwendolyn's cry when she went down.

Upon the ground, Gwendolyn saw the blade coming down on her, but blinked as it was blocked and Costentyn's face appeared instead, pulling her to her feet.

"Go!" he yelled, pointing to Einion.

Gwendolyn drew her sword and set to cutting enemy throats to get to Einion. She did not see Costentyn's face as another enemy blade plunged into his back and he collapsed beneath the stampede of panicked and fighting feet about the hall.

All the while, Caradoc stood still, his longsword loose in his hand, as if he were watching the games at a festival, removed and easy.

Gwendolyn saw a path open on the right side of the hall and rushed along it, stabbing as she went, her heart racing as quickly as it did that Samhain's night so long ago when she had fled for her life from the slaughter of the fortress rock. She wanted Caradoc dead as much as Einion did, and so when she saw his flank open as other advisors cowered behind him, she dove in.

She stabbed one man who grasped at his slashed eyes, and then another, before leaping at Caradoc's back.

But the Dumnonian tyrant spun and slapped the blade from her hand before she could do anything. His thick fist pounded her face and she tumbled down the steps onto the burning body of his fat advisor.

"You'll be my blood offering this night," he mumbled as he walked down the stairs and picked her up by the hair.

Through the blood dripping across his brow, Dagon saw Caradoc's blade resting upon Gwendolyn's neck as Caradoc sought Einion's eyes.

"No!" Einion yelled.

Dagon's dagger soared over the hearth flames and slashed Caradoc's cheek. The latter bellowed like a baited bear in the arena, and Gwendolyn scrambled away, protected by Lucius' blade on the left of the hall.

Caradoc sprang, but Einion was there, their swords crashing together instantly.

The sound was one of horror, of grunting and slashing and ripping of tunic and flesh.

Lucius and Dagon fought hard to keep the guards away, and with the help of the villagers, their numbers were dwindling slowly, giving Einion more room to seek his uncle's death.

"Fight for your rightful king!" Dagon yelled to the peasants who stood fearful at the back of the hall. "Kill your persecutors now!"

There were cries as several peasants went down beneath the blades of Caradoc's men. The people were pushed back

124

more, tested, bloodied until only a few guards remained and the fighting spilled out onto the fortress rock, beneath the light of the blood moon and scattered fires.

Lucius saw Einion tumble and slam into the ground then, and jumped to his aid, but Einion shook his head.

"No! He's mine!"

"The Gods love you, Lord Einion!" someone yelled at the back of the hall.

The sound of battle died away elsewhere, and it was only the sound of Einion and Caradoc's fight that remained as a gruesome chorus in the stinking, bloody hall.

"You can't win this, whelp!" Caradoc spat at Einion who was breathing heavily, wiping blood from a gash above his eye.

Fight, brother! Einion heard in his mind. *The time has come! I'm with you...*

Briana? Einion shook his head and realized that his sister was speaking to him from far away, beyond the mist surrounding Ynis Wytrin.

I am with you...

Einion was about to renew his attack, but then Arthrek was flung onto the floor of the hall from the side door, a dagger in his side. Clemo and Kenal also stumbled in, their faces bloody, their bodies weak from the fight. They fought hard, but gave way under the onslaught of a new group of guards from outside.

"Form a line!" Lucius yelled to the villagers nearby, and they stood before Caradoc's newly arrived men, who crashed upon the peasants like cold winter waves upon a sandy shore.

Lucius and Dagon reinforced the flagging wall of men and women fighting to shield their lord as he attacked Caradoc once more.

Lucius felt his limbs tiring, but fought on, stabbing and slashing at grimacing faces, arms, and hands.

There was a great crash and grunt, and Lucius and Dagon chanced a glance back to see Einion upon the floor with

Caradoc towering over him, swatting aside his swift, hard punches and holding his long black blade in the air for a killing arc to finish Einion.

"NO!" Gwen yelled rushing to help but slipping on the blood and stinking offal upon the paving slabs.

Neither Lucius or Dagon could pull away without being stabbed from behind.

Einion moved quickly, as if aided by some unseen force in his limbs, so that he ducked beneath the swinging blade, spun, and hacked off Caradoc's sword hand, sending it and the black sword into the flames where they sizzled and sent sparks into the rafters.

Caradoc barely made a sound, but with incredible swiftness, and ignoring the pain of blood and fire, drew his dagger from his belt and stabbed at his nephew's face.

Einion's hand went up to stop the blade, and the steel pierced right through his hand, scraping the bone of his fingers as Caradoc pushed.

Einion screamed with rage, and an overwhelming feeling of failure washed over him. But the sight of his uncle's smirking visage enraged him all the more, even as the latter pommelled him with the bloody stump of his right arm

"The Gods have cursed you, Nephew!" Caradoc yelled, blood and spittle dripping from his mouth and beard. He kicked and punched Einion again, still holding onto the dagger with his left hand. "Your father died better than you, and he was nothing!"

Einion looked up through the haze of his crimson vision at Caradoc, at the throne behind, and the fleeting memory of his dead parents, and he gripped the blade that was planted in his left hand.

Flailing, his right hand found what he had seen out of the corner of his swelling eyes - the handle of his father's longsword - and with a great cry, the blade stabbed up under Caradoc's chin and exploded out of the top of his skull.

Einion struggled to get on his feet, and let his uncle's body fall to the floor with the sword embedded in his head.

Caradoc was dead.

A cry of rage and relief erupted from Einion's throat then, as years of dammed up grief and emotion finally broke like the passing of a monstrous gale.

"AHHHHHHHHH!"

He felt Gwendolyn at his side immediately, her bloodied face and arms grasping at him, crimson tears upon her cheeks. She touched his face.

"You've done it, my love. They are avenged..." She was exhausted, and could not move to help Lucius, Dagon and the others who slashed and slew the last vestiges of Caradoc's forces. "Caradoc is dead!" she yelled. "He is DEAD!"

Almost immediately, the fighting dwindled as the enemy forces that remained broke for the door and ran, pursued by the villagers who had tasted blood, and who had suffered a lifetime of shame at the hands of those men and their slain lord.

Lucius and Dagon stopped fighting then, and turned to see Einion, propped up by Gwendolyn, with Caradoc and a whole mound of bodies about him.

They dripped with blood and gore, and their breath was ragged, lungs heaving, eyes blinking as they came out of their battle rage.

They turned to see the hall filled with the villagers, people whose faces wore masks of shock and joy, some who recognized their former lord's son, and others who had only heard stories of the young man many had thought abandoned them.

None could speak, least of all Einion.

Dagon looked around at all the disbelieving faces and left Lucius' side to walk toward Einion.

"You must sit your throne before all these people, Einion. While the body of this tyrant lies slain by your hand at your feet."

Einion blinked and looked at Dagon.

"You have fought hard for this day. Take your father's throne at last." Dagon placed his hand upon Einion's shoulder and felt him shaking. He squeezed, to steady him on one side, with Gwendolyn on the other. Then Dagon turned to the people in the hall. "The rightful lord of Dumnonia has returned!"

He stepped back down the stairs with Gwendolyn, almost tripping on the bodies, and looked up at Einion.

Einion turned to see the stone, blood-spattered throne of his ancestors and turned to face his people.

"In the name of my father, and my mother, I will heal this land of Dumnonia which I claim by right!"

The people cheered and wept at the words.

VIII

ILLAQUEATUS ANGUIS

'To Trap a Dragon'

It was a moment to be branded onto the memories of every person there.

After years of pain, desolation, and disease, the rightful ruler of Dumnonia was about to sit upon his ancestral throne. There was no thought of the Romans to the East, beyond the moorlands, not even in Lucius' mind. Among the corpses of the slain, people only looked to Einion, son of Cunnomore.

So much blood...and time, Gwendolyn thought. *It has been worth it...for this.*

She, Lucius, Dagon and all the others forgot momentarily about all the death, the losses that night, and watched as Einion placed his bloody hands upon the smooth, stone arms of the throne, and began to ease himself down.

But he could not.

Einion tried to sit, to force himself down, but something unseen prevented him.

Then, a sound echoed in the hall, painful in everyone's ears.

A hunting horn.

The blast crashed over the assembly, forcing all to their knees.

All but Lucius and Dagon.

They knew at once what it was, and who it was. They drew their swords, their eyes searching the shadows around the cowering peasants.

"What's wrong?" Gwendolyn asked. "Is it -"

Einion's eyes met hers just before he was thrown from the dais and over the fire to crash into Gwendolyn and Dagon.

Sitting upon the throne then was the dark hunter, Gwyn ap Nudd.

The dark faery's eyes burned into the people there gathered, his dire horn still shrieking from his thin lips. The note shook the hall, so much so that Lucius believed the walls might crumble around them. The lord of Annwn stared straight at Lucius, the only one standing before him, and lowered his horn.

Without a word, the hunter leapt from the throne, sweeping past Lucius with great speed, and shot out the back door of the hall and into the early dawn.

Lucius turned and ran after him.

"Lucius! Come back!" Dagon yelled.

Lucius could hear his friends yelling behind him, their footfalls in the distance, but he ignored them. So long as the dark hunter was in sight, he ran, out of the hall, careening down the deadly slopes of the fortress rock, to the footbridge over the chasm.

The lord of Annwn was faster than any foe Lucius had pursued, and were it not for the red light of early dawn, where a pale sun and red moon shared the sky around them, he would have lost his quarry in the shadows. As it was, he never lost sight of the hunter as he ran between the smouldering remains of bonfires and bodies left by the struggle with Caradoc's men.

"Come back here, coward!" Lucius yelled as he raced across the dipping bridge to the other side.

He heard the galloping of a horse, and saw the hunter riding away to the South upon his monstrous black stallion. Lucius searched about and found a saddled, brown horse tied to a nearby shed with other carts and wagons. He leapt atop the beast and whipped it so that it reared and bolted onto the moor.

Lucius had never ridden so hard and recklessly in his life, but the fury that had taken shape inside of him knew not restraint. The thought of catching the hunter and bringing him to task was all that he could think of as he charged, the reins whipping the horse's flanks.

They raced for two miles or more. Lucius did not notice. He only knew the horse beneath him was close to blown, white foam flying from the animal's gasping mouth and nostrils.

Rain began to fall, and thunder rumbled in the iron skies above the green moor.

The hunter rode hard, looking back at Lucius and blowing occasionally on his horn as if to taunt the Roman. Then he turned eastward, making for a thick line of trees.

"Lucius!"

In the distance behind him, Lucius could hear the galloping of two more horses, and his friends' voices crying out to him.

"Don't do it!" Einion yelled. "Stop!"

An image of the nymph upon the moor flashed in Lucius' mind then, and the thought of her fate, and the fates of unknown others, drowned his reason as he rode for the trees at breakneck speed.

Faster! Faster!

He came to the top of a green field that sloped away toward thick trees where the hunter disappeared. Lucius drove the beast hard all the way to the trees, but in the dim light, he noticed the drop too late and he and the horse crashed through the thicket of strangling, tripping vines to fall twenty feet into the river below.

Lucius flung himself from the saddle and landed with a crash in the shallow water far below, narrowly missing a boulder that seemed to have been left there by some great moor giant.

He could hear the hunter galloping farther downstream and turned to get the horse he had been riding.

The beast lay dead, impaled upon a fallen tree on the river bed, the blood from its wounds washing away with the flow of water.

Lucius knelt and washed the blood from his own hands, splashed his face with the cold water as if to awaken himself.

The horn sounded again, down the river.

"You are the coward, Dragon!" a voice said. "Your friends are nothing! Your family is nothing!"

Lucius charged in the direction of the voice, his sword blade out, the only bright thing in that dark corridor hidden from the sky.

Einion and Dagon's voices echoed behind him as he ran the hunter down, coming closer and closer to reaching out with his blade, until the hunter leapt forward an unimaginable distance and disappeared beyond a veil of water and deep green.

Without thinking, Lucius lunged after him, and the sound of the water, and the voices of his friends, disappeared.

Lucius lay prostrate upon the ground, surrounded by tall blades of lush grass. He was tired...so tired. The Roman felt something brushing his face then, but his lids were so heavy that he could not open his eyes immediately.

What was I doing? he tried to remember, but his head spun. An image of a mangled horse and a river flashed in his mind then, and he opened his eyes. *The hunter!*

He felt the soft fluttering again and looked to see a small creature before his eyes, prodding, staring like an overly-interested insect. Lucius thought of batting it away, but stopped when he had a closer look.

It was a tiny woman, beautiful and delicate with arms as small and lithe as a blade of dewy grass, and long red hair that fluttered around her crown like a warm tuft of feather. When she stopped moving, standing upon his hand in the grass, he noticed the long translucent wings suffused with pink and green light.

Instead of wonder, Lucius felt like weeping, and a tear crept out from the corner of his eyes.

The creature reached out to touch his temples, and he felt calm and warmth immediately.

He pushed himself to his knees.

It was then that he noticed more of the tiny creatures, an entire flotilla of different hues, urging him to rise, to walk on.

Lucius stood, his hand still gripping his sword. He looked at his hands and clothes and his eyes widened.

There was no blood, no gore upon his skin, cloak, or armour. All was clean, and bright, and dry.

"It was raining," he mumbled to himself.

Lucius! A voice like an echo beneath the waves could be heard then, and Lucius turned around, searching for the source. *Lucius! Anguis!* They came again, two voices he felt that he recognized. He turned around and around, remembering a bloody, driving river, but only seeing a broad summer field filled with wildflowers of every colour and faeries flitting all around him.

"Where am I?" he asked the tiny creature who had woken him.

She waved her arms as if he should not worry and pointed to the tree line of a board forest a short distance away.

Lucius Metellus Anguis! the voice called again.

"Dagon?" Lucius answered...remembered, barely. "Einion?"

The image of a bloody hall assaulted his mind then, of fire and death, and he made to walk away from the distant wood, but a music began then.

Music.

A sound to tempt the Gods themselves, of strings plucked so softly, so full of feeling and care, that he immediately turned back toward the wood, the sound of his friends' voices drowned out by the beauty of it.

The faery rose up to touch the dragon upon his breastplate, and then kissed his temple.

Lucius smiled and walked in the direction the faeries pointed. He walked across the green field as they followed him, bobbing up and down on the warm breeze as a swallow soars with grace and beauty through the sky.

The blade of his sword glinted brightly, casting shards of sharp sunlight ahead of him, pointing him toward the wood. For a moment, he spotted a woman's face in the blade's reflection, a woman with curling black hair and green eyes. He stopped and stared. She was sad, weeping, staring straight at him.

Lucius, she said.

But he could not place where he had seen her before, though she too was familiar.

So familiar...

He continued walking, urged on by the tiny creatures as they took him by the hands and pulled at his clothing until they reached the edge of the wood.

Ancient trees arched overhead in a great, natural basilica, and the godly music echoed throughout the branches and emerald, sun-drenched leaves of the canopy.

It was a place he believed he had never seen the likes of before, nor ever would if he were to leave.

Beautiful... he thought.

Behind the music however, there were voices, so many voices, the hushed voices of lovers and conspirators, of poets and friends. He recognized none of them, but they were persistent and untiring, not directed at Lucius, but part of the world, hidden, it seemed, within every tree and flower, mushroom, blade of grass, and shaft of soft light.

Lucius turned to the fluttering creatures behind him, but they shook their heads. They were not coming. They pointed that he should continue on his way, deeper in the twisted beauty of the forest.

Lucius walked for some time, his sword sheathed now at his back, his arms swinging gently at his sides as he roamed the hidden paths of the wood, content to do so.

At times, he struggled to think of the name he had called out, but then remembered that it was his own. Small threads of memory dangled before his psyche, but when his mind reached out for them, desperate to know, they crumbled and disappeared.

He touched the image of the dragon with outspread wings upon his chest and felt a sharp pang in his heart, and harsh feelings of forgetfulness, of failure, of hunger and thirst beyond reckoning began to emerge.

He noticed a pair of sandalled feet on the path ahead of him, and looked up quickly to see a woman standing there.

She was tall and willowy, beautiful with high cheekbones and pale, piercing eyes. Her black hair was bound with crimson ribbon into two great tresses that fell down her back to her knees which were hidden by her long red tunic.

She said nothing, but held out a silver tray with fruit and a silver cup of wine.

"What is this?" Lucius asked, stepping toward her as a ship steers itself toward a siren's song.

She did not reply, but held the platter farther out to him.

Lucius felt the pangs of hunger and thirst then. He wanted to devour the food before him - grapes, succulent figs, apples and pomegranate - but he stayed his hand.

Lucius...

That voice again.

He pulled back, the woman taking a step closer to make up the distance. The wine looked as if it would quench the greatest thirst in the world, and Lucius found himself thinking that if he had just one sip, he would be invincible.

"No!" he yelled, angry with himself for doing so.

The woman was unmoving, but she too began to take on an air as tempting as the fruit itself, her lips the colour of the wine which she now sipped as if to show him it was safe, and good.

He felt his loins stirring, but stepped back and walked quickly down another path, away from the woman. He

135

continued to follow the music then, strength returning to his limbs with every step, but still feeling as if he were in a mist, despite the bright light about him.

Maybe it's too bright? he thought. *I should have eaten something. Why didn't I eat?*

He carried on, stepping over the thick roots that criss-crossed the path from the ancient trees. They seemed to throb with life and vitality, to hold untold wisdom in their coarse strands.

He was about to step upon another one, but stopped when it moved.

From one side of the path, among the leaves of giant ferns, a serpent's head rose to face Lucius directly. It was as thick as a man, and the eyes...those eyes...they held terror and wisdom at once. The scales shivered from brown to black to green, radiating and glistening.

Lucius wanted to reach for his sword, but was unable to. The serpent did not attack, but continued to stare at him, its forked tongue jutting out to touch the dragon upon his chest, and the edges of Lucius' lips.

A moment later, Lucius found himself standing alone upon the path. He blinked and looked about, but could not see anything.

He walked farther along after that, tried to think of light in his life, of family, of love, and laughter, but as soon as the feelings or memories occurred to him, they were blown away, as if thoughts of the outside world were banished in that place.

Lucius shook his head as he walked, turning down an overgrown path that led to a small pool at the base of a waterfall. The water seemed to pour out of the sky itself, and the pool was surrounded by a small clearing where, on one side, a great beast hunched over, drinking of the water. Lucius stepped to the edge of the pool, wanting desperately to drink, but when he leaned down, the tail of the beast shot toward him, revealing the head of a snake.

Lucius fell back and saw a great lion's head turn toward him, but even as it did, the head of a great, horned goat turned from the middle of the beast's back to accuse him of intrusion. The lion continued to lap at the water for a moment before turning and walking past Lucius.

The serpentine tail snapped at Lucius, but he dodged the bite and watched the chimera disappear back into the thick forest. As he watched it go, he looked up to see a brilliant bird of red flame in the tree above.

It was watching him, curious and intelligent, wise and courageous.

"What are you?" Lucius asked, wanting very much to speak with the bird.

The animal turned its head from one side to the other, and then looked up at the sky with closed eyes, as if it were ecstatic about something. Then, it exploded in fire as brilliant as the sun, and fell in a heap to the ground at Lucius' feet.

"No!" Lucius cried, bending over the smouldering pile of ash.

He felt like weeping for what he had just seen, but then, there was movement within the remnants, and a second later a young bird more brilliant than the last pushed its way out of the ashes and shot into the sky.

Lucius jumped to his feet and watched it soar all the way into the heavens, to the stars themselves which, as it happened, he could see, even though it was daylight.

He forgot about the water of the pool then, about his thirst, and continued on his way, drawn by the music that had become louder and more soothing than he had yet heard.

After a time, the path diverged.

Down one path, the light was bright, the air clear and joyous, and there, in the middle of that path, stood the woman with food and drink. The music was clearer there, calling plainly to him, to his heart.

Lucius turned then to the other path and saw that it was darker and overgrown. There was no music, no food, and little light, but it felt familiar there.

He drew his sword once more, and took the darker path.

It felt like an eternity, the time it took Lucius to walk that dark road.

The light of the sky and summer fields was now choked by gnarled branches of coarse bark. Indeed, it seemed the only light to be found was from the blade of Lucius' sword, though there was no source to reflect off of it. He held it tightly, ready, his warrior's senses acute.

The forest was no longer alive with sounds of wildlife, and of birds. Even the sound of the harp that had drawn him so deeply into the wood was now drowned out, choked by sounds from the world of men, of hysteria, pain, blood and the clash of battle. He recognized the chorus of war and death, of laughter and weeping mingled - it was all familiar, comforting and painful.

Lucius slowed, listening - a shuffling in the undergrowth, the snap of a bowstring.

A bloody shaft buried itself in the ground beside his foot and he spun out of the way to meet the blade of an attacker. The man stank of garlic, and broken teeth sneered at Lucius through an overgrown beard.

"Metellus!" the man grunted and cried as he slashed at Lucius, again and again, the latter parrying as quickly as he could and then finally, after ducking beneath his opponent's blade, driving his sword into the man's guts and twisting.

Lucius fell back when he saw the face.

It was the face of a man he had condemned to death long ago - Brutus.

Lucius gazed down at the bloody form of his former foe, the man who had been there when Alene, his sister, had been slain in Africa.

Lucius cried out and swung his sword into the body, again, and again, and again until it was a pulpy mass upon the earth, the blood sinking into the ground as if it had never been.

Breathing heavily, feeling sick, Lucius stumbled away, flashes of painful memory coming and going in his mind, stabbing at his heart. He charged down the path, farther into the darkness until he came face to face with a tall, bearded man in a purple cloak that was too large for him, and the brown armour of a Praetorian prefect.

"You!" the man pointed at Lucius, accusing him. He wanted to pronounce death on the soldier before him, but as he made so speak again, his beard fell away from his face to reveal the raw, bloody flesh beneath. He cried out and lunged with his thick, bare hands.

Lucius ducked and drove his blade up into the pit of his arm, impaling him and crying out himself as he did so.

"Gaius Fulvius Plautianus would have ruled..." he gasped, his hand gripping Lucius' arm before he disappeared where he stood.

Lucius spat on the spot where the body had stood a moment before, and felt hatred fill his veins. He cried out, something like a roar in the wood, and lumbered down the path, blood dripping from his hands. He tripped along, his anger unbalancing him as he went, fear rising in his gut. He wanted to vomit, to cry, to fall upon his sword with every step, but he carried on in the darkness, blind.

"There you are," a voice said.

Lucius looked up from the path and saw the outline of a tall, well-built warrior in a black cloak, standing before him, unmoving.

Lucius raised his sword. "Who are you?" he said. For a moment, he thought he was looking at his own reflection, but something about the man did not feel right. "Get out of my way."

"No," the man said, the cadence of his voice registering something in Lucius' muddled mind. "You owe me, Lucius."

139

"I don't owe you anything," Lucius answered, crouching into a fighting position.

"Yes," the man said. "You do!"

Their sword blades crashed together in the darkness, the sparks lighting the path as they stabbed, punched, and pommeled each other with violent intent, each seeking the other's death.

"Fratricide!" the man said, lowering his guard, seemingly crying. "Coward! You let him kill me instead of doing it yourself!"

Lucius stopped to see the man pull back his hood.

"Ar...Argus?" Lucius' blade lowered. "Impossible. You're dead!" The memory shot back to Lucius like an arrow, the pain upon the face before him unbearable and unnerving.

"He cut me," the shade said, angry red lines appearing all over his body and across his neck. "Into little pieces." He smiled, raising his sword to strike another blow.

Lucius swung, hard and fast, and the body of his half-brother fell apart like beastly pieces upon a butcher's block. He looked down to see maggots creeping out of the earth all over the mass of flesh, eating, devouring, until it was gone, disappeared as if it had never been.

Lucius found himself shaking then, gazing at his bloody hands, the red waste upon his blade, and not knowing where any of it had come from.

He only knew a growing fear in the pit of his stomach as he walked forward, bloody and ignorant in the darkness. He wanted to weep for how he felt, but he was not sure why, only that the world of that forest was closing in on him.

At one point, after roaming for a time, the forest grew quiet, still and dour as an ancient necropolis.

Lucius walked forward, for it was the only way to go. Behind him, the path seemed to have become overgrown as he passed. He wiped his brow, blinded by the sweat that now dripped down his face. He wished now for the sound of that harp, which he could remember, and for the platter of food offered him by the silent woman. As it was, he went on, his sword blade continuously dripping, as if it had only just taken a life.

Finally, there was a light ahead.

He peered into the darkness beneath the low-hanging branches to see what looked like a thick column jutting out of the earth like a titanic white spear that had been thrown and had taken root there among those primordial trees when they were but saplings.

He approached, his hand out, and touched the smooth, white marble, so out of place in the wild darkness. It was cold, and sent a shock through his senses.

Then he heard a scraping sound above, and he looked up slowly to see two great claws curling, tightening over the edge of the top of the archaic pedestal.

Lucius stumbled back, tripping over scattered piles of bones that lay upon the path. He had not seen those on his approach. He held his sword out, but as he did so, he became aware of myriad eyes and fangs in the darkness flanking the path. He wanted to run for some high ground, but the column blocked his way, and the path behind had disappeared.

He froze and looked up again, his heart racing as he struggled to calm himself, to prepare for the death he felt was upon him.

Eyes as terrifying as any nightmare apparition, bright and cold, stared down at Lucius from a woman's face. Long, smooth hair the colour of jet hung down over her shoulders, if they could be called that, for her body was that of a graceful, quick, and deadly lioness.

The Sphinx! Lucius thought, the name for it coming to his mind.

He looked away quickly, and could hear the claws of those massive paws grip onto the ancient marble. He waited for the attack, but none came, not from the forest, not from above.

Mortal man... Look at me! a voice inside Lucius' head said.

He looked up to those eyes, and saw the great curved wings unfold above the Sphinx's body.

You cannot pass, the voice continued, the eyes bright and cold as moonlight. It was the voice of a stern woman, and yet almost motherly. There was no tenderness, no emotion, only a certainty of ages that all the Sphinx said or decided upon was truth. Lies had no power over her, nor trickery.

Lucius began to shake, and grew angry with himself, for he felt he should be otherwise, that with the sword in his hand, he was invincible. But any feelings of power or strength were sapped from his spirit as soon as they came to him.

"By the Gods, please let me pass," Lucius said, his voice more like that of a child's.

"No. Your gods cannot help you here, Roman."

Lucius looked left and then right to see the eyes getting bigger, the fangs more visible as black lips contorted above them.

"There must be a way," Lucius said.

There is, the Sphinx said, her voice an echo in his head. *You must answer my question.*

"A question?" Lucius looked up at her unmoving face.

Yes.

"Ask me," he said, finding some of his courage. He stood a little taller, and pushed back his cloak so that the dragon upon his breast reflected the light from the pillar. "I am ready."

Are you? it asked. *You must answer correctly.*

"What if I do not know the answer?"

Death.

Lucius was silent. He gazed at the column and up at the Sphinx as if he were standing at a precipice, ready to throw himself over a cliff and into oblivion. He knew he had no choice. He felt the pull of the world beyond that column. He could also feel the fangs and claws of whatever beasts stood waiting in the shadows to tear him apart.

"Ask me your question," Lucius said.

The Sphinx stood straighter now, her wings out, her claws poised. The eyes in the dark jostled and blazed as they bored into him from every side.

Who are you?

Lucius felt relief wash over him, and then...terror.

"Who am I?" he repeated.

He began to sweat then as his mind tried to grasp the enormity of the question and the outcome of a falsehood. For a moment he rubbed his chin, scratched his head, his sword handle wet in his right hand.

Every time he was about to frame the words of his answer, they slipped away, eluded him, like down or sifted flour in the wind. No matter how hard he tried, he could not think of the answer to that one, simple question. He dug, clawed desperately with both hands in the farthest recesses of his mind. He saw armies marching, cities aflame, seas of sand, and the deaths of countless men. He saw and remembered it all, but he could not, for his very life, remember who he was.

The Roman fell to his knees at the base of the column, frustrated and weeping, then screaming as he clung to the sword in his hand. He saw the dragons upon the brilliant hilt, watery through the tears in his eyes. His heart ached as if it were being torn out of his chest and he put his hand to his cuirass as if to beat out the pain racking his soul.

He was about to give in to the despair, to admit what the Sphinx already knew - that he did not know himself.

Lucius... A soft voice spoke from out of the chaos in his mind. It was like a song out of time, out of memory - his memory. *Come home to us...* A prayer of whispered words in the dark of night. *My love...my life...* A gift of clarity, not from any god, not from himself.

"Adara?"

The name remained on his lips, familiar, comforting, solid and powerful. He clenched his eyes and saw them, his wife, his children, not pain but joy, and peace, and he knew them. They were the single strand of twine he sought in the darkness of the labyrinth of his mind.

He opened his eyes and gazed at the dragons upon the sword in his hand, the sword his wife had given him, and he gripped it, and stood back to look up at the Sphinx whose eyes seemed to open even more, the claws ready to pounce.

Are you ready to die? the Sphinx's voice said.

"No," Lucius answered confidently. "I have your answer. I know who I am."

Who are you?

"I am a husband and father."

The eyes in the dark came closer but did not attack.

"I am a son, a brother, a man, and a warrior." He slowed, not wanting to misstep and risk death. "I am honourable. I am light."

The Sphinx leaned over the edge of the top of the column now, a slight expression of judgement upon her face.

"I am blessed by Apollo," Lucius said, his hand going to the great image of the dragon with outspread wings upon his breast. I am Lucius Metellus Anguis, of an ancient line blessed and cursed by the Gods for ages." He paused, looking down at his hands, now clean of blood and sweat and dirt. He looked up one last time. "I am the Dragon."

There was a pause, and Lucius waited for the attack from the sides. He thought of Adara, Phoebus, and Calliope's faces, of his friends, his warriors, and his gods.

"I am Lucius...Metellus...Anguis!"

At that moment, the eyes on either side of the road retreated into the forest, and the Sphinx stood still once again on her haunches upon the ancient column.

Lucius waited for another moment.

You may pass...Dragon.

Lucius made his way around the base of the column, sword in hand, and headed for the dim light ahead.

Adara... Thank you, my love... he thought as he pressed on. *I remember.*

It was not long before Lucius broke free of the tangle of that dark forest and found himself in a meadow exploding with flowers, birds and their song. The sun warmed him and he felt strength returned to his limbs.

Where am I?

Then the music began again, soft and lulling, pulling him forward with more power than before.

He crossed the field and came to a wide slope dotted with brilliant white birch trees whose leaves waved wildly in the warm breeze. Before him was a valley with rocky cliffs rising up on either side. The valley was lush, bright and green with a stream running through it. It reminded him of the vale of Tempe, or what he imagined that legendary place to be like.

Lucius sheathed his sword at his back, and began to climb down the steep gradient. The sky seemed to turn awkwardly above him as he went, and he had to pause several times for the dizzy feeling that crept up his neck and into his head.

The music was softer in the valley, but it was there still, an audible beacon, a goal. He felt that if he could just reach the source of that lovely music, all would be well.

He reached the bottom and set off along the path beside the small stream. Ahead, white horses emerged from the wood to drink, and then disappeared before he reached them, shy of the mortal man in their midst.

Lucius remembered Lunaris then too, and sadness crept over him once more. He stopped to sit upon a rock beside the water and watched the horses from a distance. When he had rested, he stood and set off again, but this time, the maiden with the food was there.

Again, she did not speak, but held out her tray brimming with fruit and wine.

Lucius reached out for a moment, hoping the food would ease his sadness, his longing for his family, but he stopped short again, stood quickly, and set off with the woman watching his back.

145

The valley twisted and turned much more than had appeared from above, and for much longer. Eventually, the trees thinned and the cliffs closed in on either side, making it seem as if he were walking some decumanus maximus of the Otherworld.

It was then he heard a spluttering cough, faint but recognizable.

Beyond a turn in the path was a small branch of the road that led directly to a small domus.

"There are Romans here?" Lucius said to himself.

The domus had a red door set in the middle of cracked, white walls. The tiles of the roof were cracked and overgrown with moss and dead leaves.

The cough came again, from the other side of that door.

Lucius approached, and as he got closer, he saw that the door had a rusted knocker upon it in the shape of a griffin.

"It can't be..."

Lucius reached out to touch the knocker, but it crumbled in his hand. He drew his sword and pushed the door with his left hand.

It swung open, the hinges rusty and loud.

Lucius stepped over the threshold and gasped.

He was standing in his father's tablinum back in the old Metellus domus, near the Forum Boarium. The room looked ancient and unkept, and smelled of rot and death, out of place in that otherworldly realm. The walls that had once been painted with vibrant colours of red, yellow, blue and white were now faded and crumbling. Scrolls rotted in their pigeon holes at the back wall, and scattered all about the room were the shattered, neglected remains of their ancestors' imagines.

"I am sorry," Lucius said to the faces of Numidicus, Dalmaticus, Macedonicus and the others. He bent over to pick up a fragment of a death mask that had belonged to his grandfather, Avus Metellus Anguis, and brushed the dirt from it.

"You're too late!" a voice snapped angrily. "Useless!"

Lucius jumped, nearly dropping the mask fragment, and looked up to see his father, Quintus Caecilius Metellus, sitting at the large table in the middle of his tablinum, as he always had done, hunched over papyri of accounts and ledgers, letters to others who shared his stubborn views of how the world should be.

He did not look up at Lucius, but continued scratching away at a letter. When he was finished, he dropped his stylus and looked at Lucius.

"The great disappointment finally has the courage to show himself," he said, spittle falling from his mouth as he hunched over the table. "I knew you would be a failure. Where are your gods now? Hmm?"

Quintus Metellus pushed back his stool and stood there before Lucius in a ragged, thin-striped toga that was torn across the middle. There, a wound gaped at Lucius, opening and closing, spewing blood like an unconscious drunk vomiting his lunch.

Lucius was repulsed by his father's shade.

"The bitch killed me!" Quintus Metellus said, referring to his wife. "I should have done away with her!" His lip quivered in long-nursed rage and he pointed a bloody hand at Lucius. "You let her!"

"You had Alene killed," Lucius said, wanting to draw his sword and slay him, but he knew it was a shade, a memory of the hate his father had spewed.

And yet, he is so real.

"You are to blame for your fate," Lucius told him. "You got what you deserved."

"And what is that, you cur?"

The face before Lucius was a hateful, familiar smirk. The skin seemed to rot continuously upon the emaciated body as if his shade were starved of offerings to the dead which, of course, it was.

Quintus Metellus had not earned the offerings due to him in the Afterlife, and so, this was the sad eternity he had been doomed to.

Lucius began to back away and out the door.

"Where are you going?" Quintus Metellus demanded.

Lucius ignored him, turning his back and walking back out into the green of the valley, even as his father's shade screamed and roared from inside his crumbling world.

Lucius did not look back, but stared down at the piece of his grandfather's face. He touched the kind eyes, and walked toward the stream where he placed the mask upon a boulder lit by sunlight.

"Don't listen to him, Lucius," a voice said as someone approached Lucius from the crumbling domus he had just left.

Lucius turned away from the mask quickly, his sword up, to see a man in a red legionary tunic walking toward him.

The older man was strong-limbed and calm. He moved easily, as if unburdened by pain or regret, and he smiled tenderly and with pride as he looked upon Lucius.

Lucius lowered the sword and sheathed it. "Grandfather?"

The legionary nodded. "I've been watching you, Lucius. We're all very proud."

"Who?"

"The dragons," Avus Metellus said.

"Dragons?"

"Yes. We are, all of us, proud of your deeds and efforts."

"He was never proud," Lucius nodded in the direction of the domus he had just left.

Avus pursed his lips. "He was never one of us. You should forget about him, for there is more to that part of the tale that you do not know."

"What? Tell me, please." Lucius had a sudden longing to know all, to sit and talk with his grandfather about everything he had ever wondered about.

But Avus Metellus shook his head. "It is not for me to say, Lucius." He put his hand on Lucius' shoulder, and it was warm. "You must press on."

"I don't know if I can," Lucius said, and as the words escaped his lips, the music of that world became louder, harder to resist.

Avus smiled. "You can." He removed his hand and turned to walk away into the wood. "Remember," he added, turning to Lucius once more. "You are never alone."

Lucius watched his grandfather leave, and would have followed him but for the pull of that music. He looked at the crumbling domus again, heard the yelling and coughing within, and turned away from it. He then continued on his way, leaving his anger with his father behind to die along with him.

Lucius looked up at the sky as he walked along the swift flowing stream. The sunlight seemed to be fading, but slower than was normal.

It bothered him, that place, and he fretted about how to escape it.

But how, without the Gods' help?

A part of him knew that if he but ate the food offered by the mysterious maid in the wood, all would feel well in the world, and that his worries and cares would disappear like morning mist when the sun comes out. But he suspected that if he ate or drank, he would not be able to stop.

"Keep going, Lucius," he told himself.

He picked up his pace, eyes scanning the oddly lit woods, and the gurgling waters where, he swore, he saw sea nymphs, or something like them, beneath the surface.

Then the stream broke into two channels.

The first flowed directly ahead, broader and more swift, heading straight for a cave which Lucius could clearly see. It had a carved entrance and there was a dim light in its depths. "Metellusssssss," a chilling voice called from within the cave.

Lucius froze, and looked at the alternative route.

The second channel of the stream was much smaller. It flowed away to the left and disappeared beneath an arch of emerald vines and what appeared to be rowan.

He decided on the first, and continued walking directly for the cave and the call of his name.

After a few feet, he stopped and turned, his eyes drawn inexorably to the second tributary of the stream. Something told him he should go there, as if the future depended on it somehow, if ever he were to get out of that place.

He made for the natural arch, and it seemed that the sounds of the hidden beasts of that realm rose to fever pitch as he approached.

Lucius drew his sword and peered into the darkness into which the water flowed. He stepped into the water and found it was only ankle-deep. The light was pale and grey, as of a sad, overcast sky. He stopped and listened.

The sound of birds and beasts had been sucked out of the air to be replace by a muted thrumming, and a chorus of weeping on the wind.

He felt sadness then, acute and powerful, but he continued, walking through the water as the stream widened to engulf a forest of saplings sticking out of the ground as though in a flooded battlefield after the slaughter.

When the trees ended, Lucius found himself facing a large green mound. It rose out of the lake like the ancient barrows within which the heroes of Troy had been buried.

The water lapped around his feet, and the tip of his blade which he held at his side.

Lucius pulled his cloak closer about himself.

It was a sad, quiet, and lonely place. No offerings graced the green slopes, and there was no altar upon which libations had been poured, nor blood spilled, to honour the heroes buried within. There was only mist, and cold, and the sound of weeping.

A breeze picked up, rippling the water of the lake softly, as if a goddess had breathed upon it, and the mist encircling the barrow's crown drifted away to reveal a large, thick, stone throne.

Einion? he wondered upon seeing the throne, but he knew almost immediately that this was not the throne which he had helped to set his friend upon.

Lucius squinted, tried to get a closer look, and gasped where he stood with the black water lapping at his legs.

Upon the back of that mighty seat was the image of a dragon, the same as the one upon his breast.

He looked down and then back up at the dragon upon the throne. It did not glow or appear to move, however, as his often did. Rather, it was still and aged.

As Lucius took a step closer, the dragon began to bleed, and it continued to bleed so that crimson streams stained the throne and ran into the mass of the green mound.

Slowly, with a bank of passing mist, a man appeared there upon the seat, a warrior in leather armour and mail with a dragon upon his chest. Leaning against the side of the throne, a shield with the image of a bear upon it also appeared.

Lucius wanted to call to him, a once-strong and vibrant human who now sat hunched over upon his seat, one hand upon his knee, the other upon his bearded chin. Lucius wanted to weep for the man, for in him he saw a once-proud visage, a man of purpose and of ideals, torn and wearied by the cruelties of the world.

His face told of unimaginable loss, grief, and shattered dreams. And he wept...oh, he wept.

Lucius could feel his pain acutely, as if it were himself sitting there, and for some reason he realized the man looked familiar. He looked up at the man and felt that he was out of a time and place that was utterly foreign to him in some ways, but only too familiar in others. "All will be well," Lucius heard himself say. "There will always be help."

The man looked directly at Lucius, his tears continuing to run from his wounded eyes into his beard as he shook his head.

"Yes," Lucius repeated. "All will be well... You are never alone." Then, he stopped upon seeing the glint of gold and steel beside the man's feet.

A sword? He came closer, trying to look up enough to see the blade leaning against the base of the throne where blood ran over the hilt before feeding the earth.

Lucius stopped, and felt himself shaking. He looked down at the sword in his own hand, and then back at the man's.

They were identical.

It was the same sword.

What does this mean? Lucius wondered.

The man smiled sadly at Lucius then, and leaned on his knee once more to look more closely at Lucius before a bank of mist rolled in to hide him from view.

Lucius backed away, unsure of what the Gods would show him, what they could tell him if they could speak to him in that place.

He left the lake behind, and made his way back up the stream to where it branched off.

Sadness and despair clung to him and, unsure of the reasons why, a feeling of failure and brokenness that he knew at once were felt by that lonely warrior he had just left behind.

When Lucius arrived back at the spot where the stream broke into two, he turned left and headed directly for the cave mouth, drying his tears as he went.

"Metellussssss," the voice called to him as he approached.

The mouth of the cave gaped like a great maw leading into Hades itself.

Lucius stood before it, unable to see any other path except that directly before him. Tendrils of vine hung down like oily hair before the entrance, and Lucius stepped forward to part them with his blade and peer inside.

It was dark within, dank, and stinking of mold from ages past.

And it felt familiar...unnervingly-so.

Lucius stepped in, and began to move through the dark.

He could hear creatures of some sort crawling along the walls and skittering out of his way as he walked. The air was so close that he could barely draw breath as he went with the edge of his cloak over his mouth and nose.

Then, directly ahead, a light kindled in the darkness, small at first, like a spark, and then growing in size to reveal a large bronze tripod in the middle of a small chamber carved out of stone.

Lucius approached the light, hearing familiar words whispered as he did so, words to send a chill down his spine to harry his courage.

Beloved of Apollo...
Where does your home lie?
Where does your heart lie?
Where does your sword lie?
Loyalty! Listen to the immortal!
Bravery and wisdom.
Eagles and Dragons...

Lucius dropped the hem of his cloak when he reached the fire, flushing at the sight before him, and the sound of the words echoing in his mind over and over again.

In an alcove carved into the rock sat an ancient crone. She appeared to have been there for ages, and Lucius wondered if she might be dead.

But he knew she was not.

She said nothing when he approached, only stared at the bench opposite her.

Lucius wanted to leave, to turn and flee, but he could not. He felt the pull of the seat as if something deep within the earth beneath commanded his obedience.

"Apollo?... Lord?" Lucius said as he sat, searching for his god's light in the darkness.

"Not in this place..." the crone said.

Lucius looked up and felt himself pushing backward hard against the rock wall where he sat. "It's you!" he said. "The Sibyl!"

She nodded slowly, smiled so that her toothless gums jutted behind grey, cracked lips like slivered flint.

Her voice, terrible and ancient, thrust Lucius back into the cave at Cumae, but this time, he was alone, a lost child.

She saw him remember, and smiled.

"Metellusssssssss..." she hissed.

"How do you come to be here?" he asked the Sibyl.

Her gnarled hand shot out like a viper and touched his forehead.

Suddenly, Lucius was out in the open, standing upon the earthen ramparts of his home. He looked out over the green sun-filled plains, closing his eyes to feel the sunlight upon his face, warm and welcome. Soothing.

Then, the cry of a crow in the sky, and a rush of wind so powerful it blew his hair and cloak back.

Lucius turned to see his family in the midst of a storm, Adara with a sword in hand, standing before their children as shadows closed in on them. He was about to turn and run to them, to scream, when a loud, powerful chant emerged on the wind, making the shadows about his family darker and more menacing. He cocked his ear and turned to look back over the plains below the ramparts.

"Metellus! Metellus! Metellus!"

There, upon the plain, were legions of men and cavalry squadrons, all of them looking up at him, calling out his name and raising sword and shield and spear to him.

At first, he thought they were there to attack him in his home, but then he realized, with perhaps greater fear, that they were pledging themselves to him, smiling at him, urging him to take what they offered.

"Imperator!" some men in the front ranks called.

"Ave Lucius Metellus Anguis!" called others.

Vexillia bearing the image of gold dragons upon red backgrounds fluttered in the breeze and the earth shook with the stomping of feet.

At the front were rank upon rank of Sarmatian cavalry, their sixteen foot kontoi pointing at Lucius while their draconaria roared with the building wind.

Lucius stepped forward to the edge of the ramparts and gazed over the land, the tens of thousands of men who called his name in concert.

"Metellus! Metellus! Metellus!"

It was then that he felt power surging through him, body and soul. It was then that he felt he could, with this army behind him, make right all the wrongs of the world. It was then that he realized what could be there for the taking. He had only to accept the acclamation of the legions before him.

His senses tingled and he raised his sword to the masses below.

They roared like an army of titans, invincible and daring, their courage fired by him.

"Baba!" came the desperate cry behind him.

Lucius turned to see his family being overwhelmed then, and made to run to them, but he tripped and tumbled headlong down the steep embankment with the cries of his family and his men echoing in his spinning head.

When he came to a stop, he was sitting in the dank cave, staring across at the Sibyl, her myopic, all-knowing eyes stabbing at him.

"Why do you show me this?" he demanded.

"Do you really know yourself, Metellussssss?" she asked. "I know you, and I know the outcome of the choices you have made in the world."

"Gods, help me," Lucius choked, the air getting thinner and harder to breathe. He felt his limbs shaking, even as the crone looked at him and laughed horribly.

"The Gods cannot help you here, Lucius Metellus Anguissss… But you cannot leave here without their help."

"What?" Lucius gasped. "I don't understand!"

"Your trial begins," the Sibyl said. "The Far-Shooter warned you, and now you must suffer the price."

Lucius shook his head, unable to look away from her cloaked face.

"Claw your way back to your green mound, Roman, and there die upon it!"

Decrepit hands reached out and scratched Lucius' face.

He could feel his skin tear and he stumbled out of the alcove, choking, past the fire and down the long, triangular corridor toward a distant, silver light at the very end of the tunnel.

As he went, the Sybil's cruel laughter chased him like a fury into the open where he stumbled, yearning for fresh air beneath a full, brilliant moon.

Lucius lay there, gasping like a fish that had been held captive out of water, and for several heartbeats, he lay there, his face bleeding and raw, his mind racing with terror.

It was then he sensed he was not alone, and opened his eyes.

He was in the middle of a circular grove of ancient oaks and there, before him, stood the Gods.

IX

SANGUI IN ORBEM ALIUM

'Blood in Annwn'

Lucius looked around, dizzy and still breathing quickly, but his eyes found them, those immortals to whom he prayed, who had helped him through countless battles. He faced them, speechless - Epona, Venus, and Apollo, an aura of brightness emanating from them where they stood in that moonlit grove beneath the far reaching branches of trees as old as time.

Lucius wanted to run to them, to fall upon his knees before them and be comforted, but their passive stance told him that was not possible.

"Welcome, Dragon," a smooth voice called from behind him, directly opposite his gods.

Lucius felt a chill run the length of his body as he turned slowly to face the Morrigan, that dark goddess who had haunted him since blood had been spilled in Caledonia.

"Your gods cannot help you here and now." She laughed, hideous and cold, a laughter as black as her flowing robes. Her appearance was dark and beautiful, not one of horror as in the world of men.

"Annwn is our realm," she said, nodding to Gwyn ap Nudd, the dark hunter whom Lucius remembered chasing from Einion's throne room. "The night of Samhain is my time," the Morrigan said, and in this place, your gods are bound by different laws."

Lucius looked to Epona, Venus and Apollo. "Why am I here?" he asked, sounding like a youth searching for answers.

"You are here to die," the hunter said plainly.

Lucius' blade was up in a moment, pointed at Gwyn ap Nudd. "You and I have unfinished business," Lucius said.

The dark hunter took a step forward. "Soon enough, mortal," he growled.

"This is intolerable!" Epona burst out, her red hair like fire in the moonlight. "You cannot do this!"

"It is the law," the Morrigan answered dismissively. "You!" She pointed at Lucius with a long white hand. "You attacked me upon the field of battle. Me! A goddess! And you shall suffer for it."

"You slew my men," Lucius countered, the memories of loss and blood rushing back. He turned to his gods and saw Venus with her hands clasped tightly before her, her loving eyes looking to him, trying to will strength and warmth into his body.

But Lucius felt unaltered. He bowed his head to her then, and looked to Apollo.

Lucius' patron god stood there, tall and strong, but unarmed. The stars of the heavens did not whirl in his eyes then, as they always had; they were blue, lit by the light of Annwn's full moon. The eyes met Lucius' and urged him to fight like he had never fought before.

They went to the sword in Lucius' hand.

It was subtle, a tremor only, but in that moment, Lucius felt his sword vibrate. It was like the plucking of the string of a kithara. A single note, but so beautiful and strong that it held myriad memories that rushed to Lucius' mind, including what Apollo had told him upon the road - *Keep your wife's sword close at all times.*

Apollo was still as the Morrigan began to speak again, but Lucius could see his belief in him, his urging.

This is a battle you must fight alone.

And Lucius knew it.

Epona shook her head when Lucius nodded.

"No, Lucius!" she said, and the other gods looked to her in surprise.

The Morrigan smiled. "Say farewell to your pet mortal, Cousin."

Lucius breathed deeply and turned to the dread goddess behind him. For the first time, he noticed and heard swirling masses of shadow in the trees beyond the light, jostling, crying out, cheering and jeering, their ghostly eyes all focussing on Lucius where he stood in the centre of the sacrificial grove.

"You must fight now, Dragon, without the help of your gods," the Morrigan said.

Apollo stepped forward, bright and shining to face the dread goddess. "If you do this, if you harm him, no laws of men or gods will protect you or this place, for by Olympus, I will burn all of you to ash in sun fire."

For a moment, Gwyn ap Nudd hesitated, and the Morrigan was silent.

But her smile returned. "You cannot threaten me now, for not even you are safe this night. If a mortal attacked you, sought your death, what pain would you visit upon him?"

Apollo did not answer.

The Morrigan continued. "The dragon must fight. Tonight, his destiny is his own to control, not yours to protect." She turned back to Lucius who stood there fighting every ounce of palpable fear in his body.

Apollo stepped back to Venus' side.

Lucius looked up from his sword and hands, the marks of the dragons jutting from beneath his arm guards, the gold intertwined dragons wrapped about his finger. *Adara...*

"If I refuse?" Lucius said, a last attempt.

"Then you shall never see Rome again," the dark hunter blurted.

"And if I win?" Lucius asked.

"You won't," Gwyn ap Nudd said, calmly. "You will pay for attacking the goddess, and for hampering my hunting."

"Brave god," Lucius mocked, "hunting helpless nymphs in the night."

"And now I shall kill a dragon!" Gwyn ap Nudd roared, turning to the shadows of his denizens in the dark of that Samhain's night.

Lucius gazed about, and cast a last look at Apollo, Venus, and then Epona, whose eyes pleaded with him to be strong.

"If you win, Dragon," the Morrigan said, "you may leave Annwn to go back to your insignificant life." She chuckled. If you loose here, there is no more."

"Do not push things, Morrigan!" Apollo finally said, his light bursting and driving back the shadows for a moment.

"You have no power here," she answered. "And we are wasting the moonlight. Begin!" the Morrigan said, and immediately, a drum began to thrum in the background, replacing the calm plucking of the harp that had led Lucius to that place of trial and slaughter.

Lucius drew his sword and stepped forward, settling into a fighting stance.

"I do not fight for Rome," he said as they approached and studied each other.

It did not escape Lucius' attention that Gwyn ap Nudd looked different in Annwn, almost mortal, but he would not let himself be fooled as if by a tiny, beautifully-coloured viper that begs observance.

The lord of Annwn was as deadly there as he was in the world of men, and Lucius knew that this was a fight he must win, else he would perish along with all of his hopes and dreams of a life of peace with his family.

Gwyn ap Nudd smiled. It was obvious he had never lost a battle. He was tall and lean, like a cheetah, and just as fast in attack and retreat.

It struck Lucius that he was to cross blades with a god, and that his own gods were unable to intervene, only to watch helplessly from the edge of the grove.

Apollo had warned him of this, that he could not help him once he crossed into Dumnonia.

Lucius now had to pay the price for his choice. *A choice I cannot regret,* he told himself.

He looked at his opponent. Every part of him was covered in a close-fitting armour, the texture of black snake skin that shimmered in the light.

Winged creatures fussed about the lord of Annwn, his handsome face supremely confident and calm.

But also arrogant, Lucius thought. *A weakness?* He shook his head slightly, his feet circling on the grass slowly. *Don't be fooled. His armour's otherworldly.*

The Gods were silent, but the shadows beyond the ring of moonlit trees jostled and hissed, their voices muffled in places, sharp in others, and all the while, the thrumming of the drum continued.

Gwyn app Nudd stopped circling Lucius and stood there calm, tall, his limbs limber, muscles flexing quickly beneath his scaly armour.

Lucius' sword lowered slowly to his side, and a second later, the lord of Annwn's blade, cold and clear as mountain water, shot out at Lucius' face, narrowly missing, as Lucius turned and struck back.

The sound of those two blades shivered every leaf in Annwn as the Gods watched with clenched fists.

Lucius spun and stabbed and parried desperately to strike again, but every time he attacked, Gwyn ap Nudd was somewhere else.

Though Lucius was an expert fighter after years of war, confrontation, and constant training, in this fight he reached deep for the skills he had acquired, for he had never encountered a foe such as this.

He saw the blade sweep for his legs, and jumped, flipping in the air, but did not land on his feet as a black arm shot out to grab his cloak and slam him into the grassy ground.

He rolled quickly as the blade plunged into the earth, and found his feet, only to be parrying wildly again with little chance to attack.

He saw blood running down his arms from wounds he had not noticed he received, but it was then that Gwyn ap Nudd ducked under Lucius' blade and cut into his left side, up beneath the lip of Lucius' cuirass. He went down on one knee, a cry of pain emanating from his throat to rile the shades watching them, as much as any crowd in the amphitheatre.

Lucius' blade swept up quickly, throwing Gwyn ap Nudd off kilter. He then grabbed his opponent's long black hair and slammed his knee into the lord of Annwn's face.

Lucius cried again immediately as his opponent's blade slashed across his thighs and he was kicked several feet away to land upon his back.

Gwyn ap Nudd approached, rage upon his face, his white, slender nose bleeding down past his lips.

"You will die here...now!" he roared, raising his blade with both hands.

Immediately, Lucius dove forward to catch his legs and lifted him across the grove.

"AHHHH!" Lucius yelled, dropping his prey when the pommel pounded into the back of his head before a black knee crushed his nose.

Blood-blinded for a moment, Lucius jumped away, ripping his cloak free to wipe his face in order to see.

His attacker leapt several feet for another onslaught, and Lucius spun, parrying with his blade and the arm guard of his left hand at once. Immediately he stabbed for a killing blow and there was a howl to startle even the dead, as Gwyn ap Nudd grasped his right shoulder where blood seeped through his cut armour.

"Impossible!" the Morrigan cursed, watching them. "Kill the dragon!" she commanded the lord of Annwn.

Gwyn ap Nudd rushed back at Lucius slashing, stabbing, parrying and attacking so quickly that Lucius stumbled with every motion, leaving a trail of blood along the grass where it ran down his legs from his wounds. Then Gwyn ap Nudd jumped high as Lucius ducked and rolled, his blade sweeping out to slash at Lucius' head.

The world spun, and Lucius could feel wet running down his back as he struggled to sit up and back away while his opponent grabbed still at his shoulder, changing his weapon to his left hand.

Lucius felt the back of his head, the blood rushing out, and knew he had to fight on or prepare for his death. With the last of his strength, he stood and ran, roaring like the beast upon his chest, spinning in mid flight to take off the lord of Annwn's left hand above the wrist and then slam the flat of his blade into his face.

Gwyn ap Nudd went down, face-first into the stained grass and Lucius fell on top of him, the blade of his sword upon his neck while his left hand gripped the long black hair savagely. Gwyn ap Nudd's bloody stump hammered at Lucius, but to no effect.

"I should kill you!" Lucius yelled, his rage finally coming to the surface, his anger at having been trapped, at having had to fight in that place so far from home. "You've hunted your last," he said as he was about to cut into the white neck.

"I yield, Dragon!" Gwyn ap Nudd called, sweat covering his brow as the pain of his maiming racked his body.

Lucius stared into those cold, dark eyes and knew that it would not be the last he saw of this enemy if he let him live.

"Metellus!" Apollo's voice echoed in the glade.

Lucius blinked and shook his head. Flashes of his family rushed through his mind, of eagles and omens, and battles fought and won on distant killing fields.

He was overwhelmed with all that he saw, the paths he had tread to get to that one place where he now held his blade to a single opponent's neck.

"You have won, Dragon," Gwyn ap Nudd said.

Lucius shook him and pressed his blade so that a crimson line appeared on his neck.

"Swear you will seek no retribution upon my family, me, or my friends, for this." Lucius twisted his foe's neck so that he could look into his eyes.

Gwyn ap Nudd stared at him a moment and then his eyes strayed to the Morrigan who stood tall and menacing at the edge of the shadows.

She gave no sign to him, the only expression upon her person being disappointment.

"I swear," Gwyn ap Nudd said, stubbornness and hatred etched upon his otherworldly face.

Lucius ripped himself away from the prostrate lord of Annwn, and stumbled to the centre of the grove, his head lighter by the second.

He felt his strength exhausted, and fell sideways onto the grass of Annwn, his blood flowing from his many wounds into the ground.

"He has defeated your champion!" Apollo said to the Morrigan, stepping to Lucius' side. "You must allow him to leave this place." Apollo was shining and violent then, his eyes ablaze, with Epona and Venus coming to stand at his side.

"He may leave...if he can find the way," the Morrigan chuckled. "But you must hurry, Dragon, for the veil between worlds is thickening as Samhain ends."

At that moment, Venus knelt to help Lucius up, but the Morrigan rushed forward like a shadow falling across a pool of light.

"No!" she hissed. "You are forbidden to give him aid until he is back in the mortal world." She then knelt over Lucius as Venus stepped away with great reluctance, her own anger showing upon her godly features.

"Pick yourself up...if you can, Dragon," the Morrigan teased, her voice dripping with hate and a wish for his death, the sacrifice of a dragon upon Samhain.

Venus turned on Apollo then, her eyes pleading. "How can you allow this?" she said. "He is your son!"

Lucius felt time slow to a standstill when he heard Love's voice, the words she uttered. Slowly, the life draining from his body, he turned his wide, disbelieving eyes toward his gods.

Apollo pulled away from Love's grasping hand and stared at Lucius where he bled upon the grass, his strength leaving him. He felt tears burning the rims of his brilliant eyes as he willed his thoughts and strength into Lucius' mind.

Find the will...my son...you will not perish here! You cannot! You must live!

Lucius struggled, reached for his consciousness as if he were grasping for seedlings on the wind while at full gallop. *Impossible!* he thought, no longer sure of what was real.

Lucius! Adara's voice echoed in his mind. *Come home!*

Adara! Lucius tried pushing his heavy body up, his hand still clinging to his sword, white knuckles covered in blood.

Lucius...

He heard her again, his wife, his love. He felt the desperation in her voice, the worry laced through it.

The Morrigan and Gwyn ap Nudd laughed as the spirits in the shadows beyond jostled and hooted at the bleeding man before them.

"Get up, Metellus!" Apollo said, his voice like summer thunder.

Lucius tried again, but he could feel his wounds flowing like gruesome rivers in thaw.

"Who will help you now?" the Morrigan asked, turning around to look at the shadows as Lucius groaned with the immense effort of raising himself from the ground. The face of that dread goddess was full of dark joy at the silence, but only until that silence was broken.

"I will help him!"

The voice came from the darkness beyond where a brilliant light cut its way through the shades of the dead among the trees.

All except Lucius turned to see the Boar of the Selgovae pushing the dead aside to step into the circle of trees.

"I will show him the way out of Annwn," he said again.

The Boar stood there, shining and vital, like an otherworldly Hercules. He looked to Apollo, Venus, and

Epona, and then cast a defiant glance at the Morrigan and Gwyn ap Nudd before going straight to Lucius' side.

The blue whorls upon his body shivered and shone, and the image of the great bristling boar charged across his back and chest, daring any to stop him as he went to help the bleeding Roman to his feet.

"Come, Dragon," he said in Lucius' ear. "Your family calls to you."

Lucius looked up through the haze of blood and fading moonlight. "You?" he said, finally registering the giant supporting him. "Why?"

"Because you are mighty and honourable," the Boar said. "And because you gave me aid when no other would have dared."

Lucius cringed as he hung off of the Boar's muscular arm.

"You helped me reach Annwn, Dragon," the Boar said, "And I will help you leave it."

"You will never join the Wild Hunt again, Boar!" Gwyn ap Nudd shouted, his teeth clenched against the pain of his missing hand.

The Boar stopped, looked slowly over his shoulder at the dark hunter, and shrugged. "It was shit anyway," he said before leading Lucius out of the grove and down a forest path toward a distant grey light.

Apollo, Venus, and Epona followed in a burst of light that pushed back the dark shades crowding the forest, and left the Morrigan and Gwyn ap Nudd to watch Lucius go.

"The veil will be closed before they reach it," Gwyn ap Nudd said.

"Even if he does leave Annwn today, he cannot be allowed to survive," the Morrigan said before her form burst into a flock of ravens that shot into the darkness of the forest, leaving her hunter upon the blood-soaked earth.

"We have to move faster!" the Boar said as they rushed down the path. "Come, Dragon! Don't give up!"

Lucius tried desperately to keep his eyes open, to cling to his sword on the right and the Boar's solid shoulders on the left. He could hear his name being called in the distance, as if beneath waves.

Anguis! Where are you? Lucius!

"Your friends are looking for you still, Dragon. You will see them soon. Stay with me! I see it!" the Boar cried, his voice as it had been upon the battlefield. "Just a bit farther!"

Lucius could see it, the faint, translucent glimmer of grey light in the middle of the forest path. The trees, crowded with rushing fairies, seemed to be closing in on them the faster they went, and the hole seemed to be getting smaller and more opaque.

The Boar was all but lifting Lucius off the ground in great strides now, and soon they were before the gateway.

"Thank you," Lucius said, trying to stand as his legs took his full weight again.

The Boar nodded. "You have to fight on, Dragon," he said. "Don't give up!"

Lucius nodded and, gripping his sword, turned to fall through the portal just before it closed completely.

"Lucius!!!"

He recognized Dagon's voice for a moment before it disappeared and he was enveloped in rushing water.

"Einion! He's here!" Dagon yelled from where he stood in the middle of the rushing stream. "Lucius!" he cried, reaching into the water and pulling at the edge of Lucius' cuirass.

Lucius felt himself gasping for air then, his body dragged and turned over on the sandy bank of the stream.

"Lucius!" Einion's panicked voice rang out.

Lucius' eyes opened slightly and he gazed up to see a circle of naked, black branches clawing at an iron-grey sky. Rain poured down in sheets, hurting his ears and soaking his body to wash the blood away. He tried sitting up but his strength gave way, and he collapsed upon the sodden ground in darkness.

"No!" Dagon cried.

EPILOGUS

There was a distant sound of gulls, shrill and windswept. Light crept in through a small stone window where, beyond in the grey light, rain drove hard and constant.

Voices mumbled incoherently at the verges of Lucius' mind, and then the pain started, like a wave conjured in the punishing depths of Neptune's sea. The throbbing grew more intense, and he could feel the wave approaching, his head spinning and then...

"Ahhh!" Lucius cried out in the bed where he had been laid beside a burning brazier.

"Hold him still or he'll rip his wounds open again!" a woman's voice said.

Arms and strong hands grabbed Lucius and held him down. He was dizzy, wanted to vomit, but the feeling passed him by.

"Easy, Anguis," another voice said.

Dagon?

"You're with friends now," the voice said. "You're badly wounded. You need to stay still."

"Drink this," the woman's voice said.

Lucius felt a clay cup rim pressed to his lips, and then a bitter, warm liquid poured down his gullet. He gulped and then was lowered back onto the bed. After a moment, the wave of pain and nausea ebbed away, and all went black.

"How long has he been asleep?"

"Three days."

"What does Elana say?"

"She says that he'll heal and fight another day. That he's lucky his skull was not cloven. It will take time." There was silence a moment, and then the voice spoke again. "She also said the Gods must love him."

"Wait... He's stirring."

Lucius groaned and opened his eyes a crack to see sunlight filtering in through the small window. The sound of gulls was clearer now, and the crashing of waves, wherever they were, far less obvious.

"Where...where am I?" he said.

He felt his hand gripped and someone sit beside him.

"You are on the fortress rock, Lucius Metellus Anguis, and among friends."

"Einion?" Lucius looked to see his friend sitting beside him, his face bruised, his eyes full of worry. "Did we? I mean, are you?"

"Yes, Lucius. We won. And thank the Gods we found you, else you would have died out there."

"I saw him," Lucius mumbled. "He helped me..."

"Who?" Dagon appeared over Einion's shoulder, his long hair tied back, his face also a mask of worry and battle scars.

"The Boar...I saw him...he helped me."

Einion and Dagon looked at each other and then back at Lucius.

"The Boar is dead, Lucius," Dagon said.

"Not in Annwn. I saw him...he helped me escape."

Einion stood up slowly, his hand gripping the sword at his waist. "You must rest, Lucius. Elana says that you need time to mend your wounds."

"Elana?" Lucius said the name, unsure of where he had heard it before.

"The priestess from the Sacred Pool. She arrived just as we were bringing you back here wounded."

Just then, the sound of a wooden door opening and closing could be heard, and Lucius turned his head to see the priestess standing there in her white robes with Gwendolyn who went straight to Einion's side.

"How are you, Dragon?" Elana asked.

"Stiff. I want to move. I need fresh air."

"Soon enough. The stitches need time to hold, and the ointments time to soften and heal the skin."

Lucius felt her warm hand upon his brow and he closed his eyes.

"You are a hard man, Lucius Metellus Anguis, to go into Annwn and come out again."

"Annwn?" Einion said. "You knew?"

"I saw it," Elana answered. "That is why I came here. I knew you would need me." She turned to Einion. "And I knew you had been victorious."

"But at what cost?" Einion said, looking at the ground.

"They all knew the risk they were taking, Einion," Gwendolyn said. "They sacrificed for you and for Dumnonia, so that you could heal this land."

"How many did we lose?" Lucius asked, his eyes finding Einion's in the blur of heads hovering above him.

"Not as many as we could have lost," Dagon said. "They fought bravely, our Dumnonian friends."

Lucius closed his eyes, and unwanted, images of the forest assaulted him, of the things he had seen and done in Annwn...the things he had been told...the things he had heard. He wanted to weep.

"I want to go home to Adara," Lucius said, his eyes still closed.

"You will travel soon," Elana said. "For now rest...rest, Dragon...sleep."

The hall upon the fortress rock had been cleansed and purified of the deaths that had happened there, the blood that had been shed. The iron upon the walls had been replaced by boughs of cedar and branches of rowan and yellow gorse that brightened the stone walls. Incense burned and the smell of food and beer wafted through the hall.

Upon the stone throne, Einion, the returned lord of Dumnonia, received his people one-by-one. Some of the people were familiar, most not at all, but he took each by the hand and offered them food and clothing which was given them by Gwendolyn who sat at his right hand.

On his left, upon two couches, sat Lucius and Dagon, the latter staying near to his friend. Dagon wore his newly repaired armour and a fresh cloak, but Lucius wore only a tunic, breeches, and a thick cloak of grey wool which was wrapped tightly about his body. He could feel the tight bandages beneath his clothing, and tried to ignore the intense itching of the wounds.

The wound that bothered him most was the one at the back of his head, for it reminded him how very close he had come to losing his life, losing everything.

Lucius gripped his sword in his lap and gazed at the golden dragons upon the hilt. *I would not have won with any other sword,* he thought, and a part of that thought gave him pause, made him feel weak. *What am I without the Gods' help?* He turned back to the proceedings.

Einion's people approached him with joy and relief in their hearts and words. Each brought stories of renewed growth upon the moors, of the disappearance of the plague that had massacred their loved ones, neighbours, and friends. They also told of flocks of sheep roaming freely again, and of the return of the herds of moor ponies across their lands.

All seemed well, and Lucius and Dagon were gladdened to see Einion upon the throne that had been stolen from his family so long ago, and to which he now returned to rule as a client of Rome. The administration in Isca would not care who ruled in Dumnonia, so long as the region was stable, and loyal to Rome.

However, Lucius felt, somehow, that Rome's reach could not truly extend to this remote corner of Britannia, across the river at Isca.

This land is different, he thought.

A great sadness had come over him since he had regained consciousness, and it made him feel vulnerable. It was as if being in Annwn had sapped his strength, his will, as if the people he had seen and met, the shades who had haunted him there still clung to him. And then there were the words he had overheard, spoken by Venus to Apollo. Desperate words. Words that turned his world upside down and destroyed his sense of self.

I won't speak of it to anyone else, he swore to himself.

Even with Dagon beside him, their quest fulfilled with Einion re-united with his people, Lucius felt isolated at that moment. There was only one place he wanted to be.

He leaned over, wincing at the pain, and touched Dagon's arm.

"What?" Dagon whispered.

"We leave tomorrow," Lucius said.

"You sure you can travel?"

"I'll travel. I have to."

Dagon nodded, and turned to see Arthrek standing before the throne with a cup raised to Einion.

"To our returned lord, Einion, son of Cunnomore!" Arthrek called out in the hall.

"Lord Einion!" everyone cheered and drank as drums and flutes were pulled out and song rang through the hall.

Lucius smiled and stood slowly, wavering on his feet a little before finding his balance.

Dagon stood too, and helped him out the side door to go back to their billets on the fortress rock and pack up their things.

The morning was quiet on the other side of the causeway. Cold mist rolled off of the moors toward the sea to spill over the cliffs, and ravens cawed in the branches of the trees.

Lucius stood there with his hood over his head, securing his sword to the saddle of the horse Einion had given him. It was a large black moor pony, solid and sure-footed, with an easy gait that would not jar his wounded body. Lucius pat the beast on the head and it nudged him, the big eyes opening and closing calmly, as if he had just been woken from his sleep.

After saddling his own horse, Dagon secured their things, including Lucius' armour, to a third horse that Einion had given them to carry the provisions.

They heard footsteps coming up the rocky path and turned to see Einion and Gwendolyn approaching.

"Are you sure we can't ride with you?" Einion said. "I would see you safely home."

"You need to stay here, my friend," Lucius said. "You have only just returned to your lands, and your people need you."

Einion looked about the land, the fortress rock looming at their backs, and inhaled the salt-sea air. "It still doesn't feel real," he said, gripping Gwendolyn's hand.

"It is real," Dagon said. "You're home, and you have reclaimed your family's honour."

"I could not have done it without you both," Einion said.

"Are you sure you won't stay longer?" Gwendolyn asked. "We owe you both so much, and you are not yet fully healed."

Lucius shook his head. "No. There is only one thing that will heal me now. I need to see my family."

"And I would like to get back to Briana," Dagon said, smiling. "Do you have a letter for me to give to her, Einion?"

"Yes," Einion pulled a folded papyrus from the folds of his cloak and looked at it. He missed Briana greatly, but knew she was where she was needed. "Give her this, and tell her all that happened here. Give her my love. When she is ready to come here, she may."

"I'll look after her," Dagon said, patting Einion's shoulder.

Einion laughed. "Yes, but who will look after you?"

They all chuckled.

"We should get going," Lucius said.

"You know the way?" Einion asked. "The maps are clear enough?"

"Yes," Lucius said. Once we're across the moor and reach the sacred pool, we'll be able to find the old Roman road."

"Elana said that you may stop at her home on the way," Gwendolyn added.

Lucius nodded.

Einion stepped forward and put his hands gently on Lucius' shoulders.

"I will never forget what you've done for me and my people, Lucius. Never."

Lucius said nothing, but gripped Einion's hand, and smiled at Gwendolyn. "If there is to be a wedding, you let us know," he said, before turning to step onto a rock to mount the black pony.

He eased himself down onto the saddle and felt the wounds on his thighs pull before settling.

Dagon hugged both Einion and Gwendolyn and mounted his big horse, the rope leading the pack horse in his left hand.

"Farewell friends," Einion said, a pang in his heart at their leaving. "May the Gods guide you safely home."

Lucius and Dagon set off slowly up the road that led onto the moors and Einion and Gwendolyn walked forward to watch them go.

As the two men rode away, villagers who had been staying in tents in the fields on either side of the road came forward to thank the two warriors who had aided their lord.

Dagon smiled and nodded to them, but Lucius stared straight ahead, only seeing the road and the distance between himself and home.

"His injuries are terrible," Einion said to Gwendolyn as they watched Lucius and Dagon disappear.

"His wounds will heal. Elana is highly skilled."

"It's not his physical wounds I worry about," Einion said, his eyes blurring a little as he gazed up the mist-enfolded road. "He is changed."

On a distant peak, far away from the prying eyes of men, the branches of a lone tree shivered in the breeze at the top of the world. The sun was bright and warm, and the spot was as far from the misery of the mortal world as could be.

There, beneath the wide limbs of that tree, Apollo and Venus stood looking down with their starry eyes to the land of Dumnonia to see the two horsemen riding across the cold moors.

Venus sighed and leaned against the tree's trunk, pressing her pure white cheek to its smooth bark.

"I worry for him," she said. "The Morrigan will not leave Lucius or his family alone, will she?"

Apollo shook his head as he stepped to the very edge of the precipice, the wind rising up from below, tossing his sky-blue cloak about him. He held his silver bow tightly in his hand, ready to kill any who threatened Lucius on his way home.

"He is shaken," Apollo said. "We should have helped him more."

Venus turned to him in surprise. "It was his decision to help his friends, and he must live with that. If we were to break the godly laws, we would be nothing but oblivion."

"I know!" Apollo said quickly, and there was a peel of thunder in the blue skies about them. He took a breath, and was calm again.

"He now bears a burden in his heart that is too heavy for him - all that he saw in that other world, it is too much." Venus stood beside Apollo and together they gazed down through the clouds to see Lucius and his friend crossing the river and leaving Dumnonia.

"I did not want him to know the truth so soon, but I cannot change what happened," Apollo said. "It is what is to come that worries me now. War is coming again, and Lucius will have difficult choices ahead of him. His foes are mustering too."

"And we will be there this time. We two, and the horse goddess who loves him." Venus said, laying her hand upon Apollo's thick forearm. "He will not be alone."

Apollo nodded, his eyes watching Lucius until he reached his home once more.

Lucius and Dagon rode in sunlight, and some days after leaving the sacred pool where the priestess, Elana, had first given them aid, they found the faded end of the old Roman road. Like Theseus and the end of the thread, they clung to it until they found their way out of the labyrinth of Dumnonia.

It felt an age since they had been in that land, and when the smokey walls of Isca came into view, they stopped to look upon them.

"I never thought I would be so glad to see a Roman town," Dagon said.

"I just hope they let us through," Lucius added, nudging his pony forward. "If those Praetorians informed on us, then we could be arrested as soon as we get to the city."

"Maybe we should head north, then, try and find another way?"

Lucius shook his head. "They would find us, and a detour will take us longer to get home. It's in the Gods' hands now." *Apollo, guide us safely home.*

They reached the bridge over the river and saw that a mass of Roman troops and civilians were gathered outside the western gate.

"Whats' going on there?" Dagon said.

"I don't know, but we'll find out."

They rode across the bridge and up the road that led to the gate. It was then that one of the soldiers ordered them to stop.

"Let me talk," Lucius said.

They reined in their horses and a young optio came toward them.

"Where have you two come from then, eh?" he pointed his hastile's brass orb at Lucius' face.

"We just travelled across the moors. We're soldiers on leave. Been hunting," Lucius said.

"You don't look like you've been hunting. Where's your quarry?" the optio asked.

Lucius was about to speak when a big, familiar voice called to him from the crowd of excited villagers.

"Praefectus!"

Centurion Flaccus called to Lucius and came striding over to them.

"Stand down, Optio," he told the younger man. "This is Praefectus Lucius Metellus Anguis."

All heads turned toward Lucius and there were several murmurs from the villagers.

"That's him!" someone said. "The dragon who killed the wyrm!"

The young optio turned to Lucius in shock. "You're the dragon? Forgive me, sir, I mean, Praefectus. I didn't know. I mean, well...we've heard so much about you these last days and more."

Lucius looked toward Flaccus.

"It's true, Praefectus. Folk been coming out of the moors saying the wyrm is dead, killed by a dragon, and that the pestilence is gone. Traffic is flowing again across the river." He smiled at Lucius and stepped closer. "Looks like you've been busy."

"I suppose we have," Lucius said cautiously, seeing all the eyes gazing at him, looking for any unfriendly faces. "We've had a tough fight, Centurion, but I'd rather folk didn't talk about it."

"I hear you, Praefectus," Flaccus said, and then leaned in so that only Lucius and Dagon could hear. "Don't you worry about those Praetorians that were following you weeks ago. We took care of them. They won't be bothering you again, I can promise you that."

Lucius nodded, wary of what the murder of several Praetorians might mean if someone found out.

"I thank you, Flaccus. But the fewer who know about it, the better."

Flaccus touched the side of his nose and winked. "Understand you, Praefectus. You have my word." The centurion turned to lead Lucius and Dagon through the crowd to the gates of the city. "You need anything, Praefectus, before you set out for home?"

"Nothing, Centurion. But you have my thanks."

"Think nothing of it, sir. We're happy to serve."

There was something in Flaccus' eyes that made Lucius uncomfortable then, a sort of determined allegiance that he had not earned to his mind. It was almost conspiratorial, and he saw it in the eyes of every trooper that had crowded around the gate and upon the ramparts as he passed through.

Then the chant started, low and rumbling, before reaching a fever pitch when joined by the villagers.

"Metellus! Metellus! Metellus!"

Lucius nodded and led his pony up the street with Dagon following behind. They did not stop this time, but by-passed the forum and made straight for the eastern gates and the road beyond.

When the walls of Isca were safely behind them, Dagon pulled up beside Lucius.

"What was that all about?" he asked.

"I don't know, Dagon. But I don't like it."

"It's almost as if you went into Dumnonia a dragon, and have come out a god, from the way they looked at you."

"Don't even say that," Lucius said. *Gods help me,* he thought, remembering Annwn and the sea of warlike faces chanting his name to the skies.

It was the ninth hour of daylight on the third day of December when Adara felt herself shaken awake by her son.

"Mama! Mama!" Phoebus said.

"What is it? What is wrong, Phoebus?"

"Baba and Dagon...they're back!"

Adara felt her heart leap and swung her feet off of the couch that stood before the central hearth of the wooden hall.

She ran to the peg where her cloak hung and she and her son ran out into the daylight and down the slope to the southwest gate where Briana and Calliope stood gazing out across the fields.

"It is true?" Adara asked Briana.

"Yes. It's them!" Briana said. "But I don't see my brother."

Mingled fear and elation gripped them all as they watched Lucius and Dagon ride slowly up the slope of the road.

"I don't see Lunaris," Calliope said, squeezing her mother's hand tightly.

Adara could not speak, so worried was she for all the dreams she had had. *Such horrible dreams...*

The four of them ran down the slope, followed by Barta who had ever been their shadow.

"Baba!" Phoebus and Calliope yelled as they skipped down the slope ahead of their mother.

Lucius waved, and felt like weeping at the sight of his family, safe and sound. *Thank you, Gods, for watching over them.*

Dagon jumped out of his saddle and ran toward Briana, sweeping her up in his arms.

"Einion? Is he..." she could not ask the question, so afraid she was.

"He sits upon your father's throne!" Dagon told her. "It was a victory!"

Briana buried her head in his shoulder and wept tears that had long been held at bay.

Dagon held her tightly, kissing her wet cheeks and hair, and nodding to Barta who stood by smiling with relief at his own returned lord.

Lucius still sat in his saddle, watching them all, scanning the ramparts of their home and casting up a prayer for his safe return. He had always told Adara what happened to him on campaign, the horrors he had witnessed. In a way, it had always made things more real. But this time, he reminded himself that he could not tell her.

"Barta," Dagon said. "Help Anguis out of his saddle. He is wounded."

Barta rushed to Lucius' side and helped him out of the saddle before taking the reins of all three horses.

"Barta," Lucius said, wincing. "It's good to see you, my friend."

The big Sarmatian said nothing, but observed Lucius' weakened state with sadness and dismay.

The children ran up to Lucius and hugged him.

He ignored the pain that caused, and enjoyed the warmth of their arms about his limbs, the smell of their hair, and glow of their eyes. He saw them looking for Lunaris, but could not bring himself to tell them right away. He turned to Adara who approached him with such worry and sorrow.

"I feared I wouldn't see you again," she said, putting her arms around him and holding him close and quiet.

"I know," he said. "But I'm home now. I've come back."

She let go and kissed his mouth. She saw the scars upon his face, the worn look in his eyes and fought hard to hold back her tears.

"Thank the Gods you're safe," she said. "My love…" She looked up at him and knew that his mind was awhirl with myriad thoughts. "Lunaris?" she asked quietly.

Lucius shook his head.

"Come. Let's all go inside. There is a fire, and food, and a warm bath for each of you."

Dagon and Briana went first, followed by Adara, Phoebus, and Barta with the horses.

Lucius stood there a moment, gazing to the village in the field below, down the road, and into the distance.

What will become of us? he wondered.

Then he felt a small hand grasp his fingers.

Calliope stood beside him, her big eyes gazing up at him, tears upon her cheeks as she had realized Lunaris was not coming back.

"Come inside, Baba. Being home will help make things right again," she said.

Lucius bent over and kissed her head.

"I love you, my girl."

"I love you too, Baba."

They walked up the slope to where Adara was watching and waiting.

"Come," she said, taking Lucius' other hand. "There is much to tell…"

The End

Thank you for reading!

Did you enjoy *The Stolen Throne*? Here is what you can do next.

If you enjoyed this adventure with Lucius Metellus Anguis, and if you have a minute to spare, please post a short review on the web page where you purchased the book.

Reviews are a wonderful way for new readers to find this series of books and your help in spreading the word is greatly appreciated.

If you would like to find out what happens to the Metelli, the story will continue in *The Blood Road*. More Eagles and Dragons novels will be coming soon, so be sure to sign-up for e-mail updates at:

https://eaglesanddragonspublishing.com/newsletter-join-the-legions/

Newsletter subscribers get a FREE BOOK, and first access to new releases, special offers, and much more!

To read more about the history, people and places featured in this book, check out *The World of The Stolen Throne* blog series at https://eaglesanddragonspublishing.com/the-world-of-the-stolen-throne/.

Become a Patron of Eagles and Dragons Publishing!

If you enjoy the books that Eagles and Dragons Publishing puts out, our blogs about history, mythology, and archaeology, our video tours of historic sites and more, then you should consider becoming an official patron.

We love our regular visitors to the website, and of course our wonderful newsletter subscribers, but we want to offer more to our 'super fans', those readers and history-lovers who enjoy everything we do and create.

You can become a patron for as little as $1 per month. For your support, you will also get loads of fantastic rewards as tokens of our appreciation.

If you are interested, just visit the website below to go to the Eagles and Dragons Publishing Patreon page to watch the introductory video and check out the patronage levels and exciting rewards.

https://www.patreon.com/EaglesandDragonsPublishing

Join us for an exciting future as we bring the past to life!

AUTHOR'S NOTE

Ever since I mentioned Einion and Briana's back-story in *Warriors of Epona*, I have wanted to write a book about it. However, *Isle of the Blessed* did not seem the place to tell it, for it would have taken the story too far off course, and risked the reader getting lost, as if in the otherworldly forests of Annwn.

That is why I decided to write *The Stolen Throne* as a separate book that was released at the same time as *Isle of the Blessed*, so that the reader would not be left with frustrating questions about what happened to Lucius when he left for Dumnonia with Dagon and Einion.

In a way, this was a very different story to get into, as Lucius and his companions were beyond the world of Rome. Dumnonia is utterly foreign to other places in the Roman Empire where the Eagles and Dragons series has taken place thus far. And as Arthurian studies has always been my academic focus, this seemed like a good opportunity to explore some new themes.

Those of you with a knowledge of Arthurian lore will recognize the theme of the land suffering without its rightful ruler, a theme that is strong in Celtic and Arthurian myth. The idea that a land with a good king thrives, while a land ruled by an unlawful and wicked king, or a wounded king, falls into ruin and despair, is a common archetype in ancient Celtic literature. Hence, the wasteland that Lucius, Dagon and Einion find when they come into Dumnonia, the ancient land that encompasses part of Somerset, and all of Devon and Cornwall.

In Cornwall, several of the ancient sites visited in this story are also strongly associated with Arthurian lore, including Dozmary Pool (the Sacred Pool) where the sword Excalibur was said to have been thrown after Arthur's death, Arthur's Hunting Lodge (also named 'Arthur's Hall') on Bodmin Moor, where they slay the wyrm, and the river at

Slaughter Bridge (one of the possible locations of Arthur's last battle), where Lucius chases Gwynn ap Nudd and enters into Annwn. Then, of course, there is Tintagel castle, the fortress rock where Einion's ancestral home was located, and where, in legend, Arthur was born.

To learn about the history and archaeology of the places visited in this book, readers will want to check out the blog series, *The World of The Stolen Throne* on the Eagles and Dragons Publishing website.

I travelled extensively in Cornwall for research some years ago, and in visiting all of the sites mentioned above, I fell in love with that magical landscape. Truly, Cornwall is unlike any other place. When you walk upon the broad expanse of the moors, with ancient standing stones jutting out of the ground and rocky tors bubbling on the horizon, you really do feel like you've left the mortal world behind.

From the moment I immersed myself in that wild and dramatic landscape, I was compelled to set a story there. I did take some poetic license in some instances, such as the description and layout of Tintagel castle in the early third century, but I think it works well for this story.

As for the Romans in Dumnonia, there is little to no evidence of Roman activity to the west of Isca (modern Exeter) apart from a couple of forts near Okehampton and Nanstallon, and a Roman road marker close to Tintagel. There was some mining activity too, but, for the most part, the Romans were not very active in Dumnonia. This allowed me to make those lands something of a mystery in this story. When Lucius and his friends crossed the river at Isca, they were heading into an unknown realm.

But the Dumnonian landscape of modern Cornwall is only one of the two settings in which *The Stolen Throne* takes place. The other setting is, of course, the Otherworld, which is Annwn in Celtic and Arthurian lore.

This was perhaps one of my favourite episodes to write as it is a crucial point in Lucius Metellus Anguis' own hero's journey.

As with other heroes such as Odysseus, Hercules, and Aeneas, a journey to the Otherworld, or Underworld, is prerequisite.

The Stolen Throne is Lucius' journey to that dreaded place.

As far as Lucius' foes in this story, we have already met the Morrigan, the Celtic goddess of war and death, in *Warriors of Epona*. However, Gwynn ap Nudd, the 'hunter', is new to the story. Traditionally, Gwynn ap Nudd was the guardian of the gates of Annwn, as well as the leader of the Wild Hunt, which was said to take place every Samhain's eve, the ancient Celtic New Year which, today, we celebrate as Halloween. He is a god of the Underworld in Celtic myth, and a terrible enemy for Lucius to clash with.

Of course, one of the big revelations in this story is related to Lucius' true parentage, which was only slightly hinted at in *The Dragon: Genesis*, and *Isle of the Blessed*.

I debated making Lucius a son of Apollo. Truthfully, I wondered if readers would shun the idea. But then I thought of all of the Romans, and indeed Greeks and Trojans of mythology, who claimed divine descent. Alexander the Great believed he was a son of Zeus and descendant of Achilles. Julius Caesar claimed descent from Venus, and Mark Antony from Hercules. The difference between them and Lucius is that they actively promulgated the idea of their divine ancestry, whereas Lucius is shocked by the revelation. His world is quite literally turned on end by the knowledge. Whether he believes this about himself, and how he deals with this new knowledge, will be explored in the next Eagles and Dragons book, *The Blood Road*.

The ending of the previous book, *Isle of the Blessed*, is bittersweet, and so it is my hope *The Stolen Throne* is a worthy addition to the series. As readers, I hope that you have enjoyed it as much as I have enjoyed researching and writing it.

There is more to come, and I'm definitely excited to share the next part of the journey with all of you.

Adam Alexander Haviaras
Toronto, 2019

Glossary

aedes – a temple; sometimes a room

aedituus – a keeper of a temple

aestivus – relating to summer; a summer camp or pasture

agora – Greek word for the central gathering place of a city or settlement

ala – an auxiliary cavalry unit

amita – an aunt

amphitheatre – an oval or round arena where people enjoyed gladiatorial combat and other spectacles

anguis – a dragon, serpent or hydra; also used to refer to the 'Draco' constellation

angusticlavius – 'narrow stripe' on a tunic; Lucius Metellus Anguis is a *tribunus angusticlavius*

apodyterium – the changing room of a bath house

aquila – a legion's eagle standard which was made of gold during the Empire

aquilifer – senior standard bearer in a Roman legion who carried the legion's eagle

ara – an altar

armilla – an arm band that served as a military decoration

augur – a priest who observes natural occurrences to determine if omens are good or bad; a soothsayer

aureus – a Roman gold coin; worth twenty-five silver *denarii*

auriga – a charioteer

ballista – an ancient missile-firing weapon that fired either heavy 'bolts' or rocks

bireme – a galley with two banks of oars on either side

bracae – knee or full-length breeches originally worn by barbarians but adopted by the Romans

caldarium – the 'hot' room of a bath house; from the Latin *calidus*

caligae – military shoes or boots with or without hobnail soles cardo – a hinge-point or central, north-south thoroughfare in a fort or settlement, the *cardo maximus*

castrum – a Roman fort

cataphract – a heavy cavalryman; both horse and rider were armoured

cena- the principal, afternoon meal of the Romans

chiton – a long woollen tunic of Greek fashion

chryselephantine – ancient Greek sculptural medium using gold and ivory; used for cult statues

civica – relating to 'civic'; the civic crown was awarded to one who saved a Roman citizen in war

civitas – a settlement or commonwealth; an administrative centre in tribal areas of the empire

clepsydra – a water clock

cognomen – the surname of a Roman which distinguished the branch of a gens

collegia – an association or guild; e.g. *collegium pontificum* means 'college of priests'

colonia – a colony; also used for a farm or estate

consul – an honorary position in the Empire; during the Republic they presided over the Senate

contubernium – a military unit of ten men within a century who shared a tent

contus – a long cavalry spear

cornicen – the horn blower in a legion

cornu – a curved military horn

cornucopia – the horn of plenty

corona – a crown; often used as a military decoration

cubiculum – a bedchamber

curule – refers to the chair upon which Roman magistrates would sit (e.g. *curule aedile*)

decumanus – refers to the tenth; the *decumanus maximus* ran east to west in a Roman fort or city

denarius – A Roman silver coin; worth one hundred brass *sestertii*

dignitas – a Roman's worth, honour and reputation
domus – a home or house
draco – a military standard in the shape of a dragon's head first used by Sarmatians and adopted by Rome
draconarius – a military standard bearer who held the draco

eques – a horseman or rider
equites – cavalry; of the order of knights in ancient Rome

fabrica – a workshop
fabula – an untrue or mythical story; a play or drama
familia – a Roman's household, including slaves
flammeum – a flame-coloured bridal veil
forum – an open square or marketplace; also a place of public business (e.g. the *Forum Romanum*)
fossa – a ditch or trench; a part of defensive earthworks
frigidarium – the 'cold room' of a bath house; a cold plunge pool
funeraticia – from *funereus* for funeral; the *collegia funeraticia* assured all received decent burial

garum – a fish sauce that was very popular in the Roman world
gladius – a Roman short sword
gorgon – a terrifying visage of a woman with snakes for hair; also known as Medusa
greaves – armoured shin and knee guards worn by high-ranking officers
groma – a surveying instrument; used for accurately marking out towns, marching camps and forts etc.

hasta – a spear or javelin
horreum – a granary
hydraulis – a water organ
hypocaust – area beneath a floor in a home or bath house that is heated by a furnace

imperator – a commander or leader; commander-in-chief
insula – a block of flats leased to the poor
intervallum – the space between two palisades
itinere – a road or itinerary; the journey

lanista – a gladiator trainer
lemure – a ghost
libellus – a little book or diary
lituus – the curved staff or wand of an augur; also a cavalry trumpet
lorica – body armour; can be made of mail, scales or metal strips; can also refer to a cuirass
lustratio – a ritual purification, usually involving a sacrifice

manica – handcuffs; also refers to the long sleeves of a tunic
marita - wife
maritus - husband
matertera – a maternal aunt
maximus – meaning great or 'of greatness'
missum – used as a call for mercy by the crowd for a gladiator who had fought bravely
murmillo – a heavily armed gladiator with a helmet, shield and sword

nomen – the gens of a family (as opposed to *cognomen* which was the specific branch of a wider gens)
nones – the fifth day of every month in the Roman calendar
novendialis – refers to the ninth day
nutrix – a wet-nurse or foster mother
nymphaeum – a pool, fountain or other monument dedicated to the nymphs

officium – an official employment; also a sense of duty or respect
onager – a powerful catapult used by the Romans; named after a wild ass because of its kick

optio – the officer beneath a centurion; second-in-command within a century

palaestra – the open space of a gymnasium where wrestling, boxing and other such events were practiced

palliatus – indicating someone clad in a pallium

pancration – a no-holds-barred sport that combined wrestling and boxing

parentalis – of parents or ancestors; (e.g. *Parentalia* was a festival in honour of the dead)

parma – a small, round shield often used by light-armed troops; also referred to as *parmula*

pater – a father

pax – peace; a state of peace as opposed to war

peregrinus – a strange or foreign person or thing

peristylum – a peristyle; a colonnade around a building; can be inside or outside of a building or home

phalerae – decorative medals or discs worn by centurions or other officers on the chest

pilum – a heavy javelin used by Roman legionaries

plebeius – of the plebeian class or the people

pontifex – a Roman high priest

popa – a junior priest or temple servant

primus pilus – the senior centurion of a legion who commanded the first cohort

pronaos – the porch or entrance to a building such as a temple

protome – an adornment on a work of art, usually a frontal view of an animal

pteruges – protective leather straps used on armour; often a leather skirt for officers

pugio – a dagger

quadriga – a four-horse chariot

quinqueremis – a ship with five banks of oars

retiarius – a gladiator who fights with a net and trident

rosemarinus – the herb rosemary

rusticus – of the country; e.g. a *villa rustica* was a country villa

sacrum – sacred or holy; e.g. the *via sacra* or 'sacred way'

schola – a place of learning and learned discussion

scutum – the large, rectangular, curved shield of a legionary

secutor – a gladiator armed with a sword and shield; often pitted against a *retiarius*

sestertius – a Roman silver coin worth a quarter *denarius*

sica – a type of dagger

signum – a military standard or banner

signifer – a military standard bearer

spatha – an auxiliary trooper's long sword; normally used by cavalry because of its longer reach

spina – the ornamented, central median in stadiums such as the Circus Maximus in Rome

stadium – a measure of length approximately 607 feet; also refers to a race course

stibium – *antimony*, which was used for dyeing eyebrows by women in the ancient world

stoa – a columned, public walkway or portico for public use; often used by merchants to sell their wares

stola – a long outer garment worn by Roman women

strigilis – a curved scraper used at the baths to remove oil and grime from the skin

taberna – an inn or tavern

tabula – a Roman board game similar to backgammon; also a writing-tablet for keeping records

tepidarium – the 'warm room' of a bath house

tessera – a piece of mosaic paving; a die for playing; also a small wooden plaque

testudo – a tortoise formation created by troops' interlocking shields

thraex – a gladiator in Thracian armour

titulus – a title of honour or honourable designation

tor – Celtic word for a hill or rocky peak
torques – also 'torc'; a neck band worn by Celtic peoples and
adopted by Rome as a military decoration
trepidatio – trepidation, anxiety or alarm
tribunus – a senior officer in an imperial legion; there were six
per legion, each commanding a cohort
triclinium – a dining room
tunica – a sleeved garment worn by both men and women

ustrinum – the site of a funeral pyre

vallum – an earthen wall or rampart with a palisade
veterinarius – a veterinary surgeon in the Roman army
vexillarius – a Roman standard bearer who carried the *vexillum*
for each unit
vexillum – a standard carried in each unit of the Roman army
vicus – a settlement of civilians living outside a Roman fort
vigiles – Roman firemen; literally 'watchmen'
vitis – the twisted 'vinerod' of a Roman centurion; a
centurion's emblem of office
vittae – a ribbon or band

ACKNOWLEDGEMENTS

There are several people to whom I am deeply indebted, and who have helped me in some way along the journey of creating this novel.

I owe much to the work of Geoffrey Ashe, one of the eminent Arthurian scholars of our age. His work was my constant companion for much of this book, and his *Traveller's Guide to Arthurian Britain* was ever in my pocket as I explored the wilds of Cornwall, helping me find some of the more remote sites.

A deep debt of gratitude goes to Professor Ann Dooley of the Celtic Studies Department at the University of Toronto during my time there. She was the one who opened my eyes to the world of Celtic mythology and the richness of those traditions. She also taught me how to correctly pronounce the words of the ancient language of the Britons.

I would like to thank the welcoming staff at King Arthur's Great Halls in the village of Tintagel, Cornwall and the group of like-minded folks in the Fellowship of the Knights of the Round Table of King Arthur there, of which I was a member for a while. The shared love of Arthuriana is a wonderful thing, and it was the stone throne in King Arthur's Great Halls that was the inspiration for the throne of Dumnonia in the story.

As ever, many thanks to my editors at Eagles and Dragons Publishing, Angelina and Jeanette, for being so thorough, and to my cover designer, Laura, for coming up with another stunning work of art. And to Costis Diassitis goes my sincere thanks for all his help, as usual, with my sometimes flawed Latin. Thank you all.

I also offer much gratitude to my friends Jean-Francois and Heather Lamontagne for their constant enthusiasm and support of this series. It is a great comfort and privilege to have such friends and champions.

Of course, I am deeply grateful to my wonderful patrons at the time of publication. Thanks to J Dagger, A Diassiti, Dig it with Raven, Mayra Bone Voyage, and 'super fan', Bonnie Miller. The faith you all show in the work I do is always deeply appreciated.

As always, with every word I write, I offer my deep love and gratitude to my brilliant daughters, Alexandra and Athena, whose enthusiasm and ideas are always encouraging, and to my wonderful wife, Angelina, who trekked through the Cornish wind and rain in January to explore all of the sites in this novel. I couldn't ask for a better companion for travel and life and large.

Finally, I would like to thank my mother, to whom this book is dedicated. Long ago, you opened my eyes to the mystical and spiritual side of life, and for that, the world has been a much richer and brighter place. Thank you.

Adam Alexander Haviaras
Toronto, 2019

ABOUT THE AUTHOR

Adam Alexander Haviaras is a writer and historian who has studied ancient and medieval history and archaeology in Canada and the United Kingdom. He currently resides in Toronto with his wife and children where he is continuing his research and writing other works of historical fantasy.

Other works by Adam Alexander Haviaras:

The Eagles and Dragons series

The Dragon: Genesis (Prequel)

A Dragon among the Eagles (Prequel)

Children of Apollo (Book I)

Killing the Hydra (Book II)

Warriors of Epona (Book III)

Isle of the Blessed (Book IV)

The Stolen Throne (Book V)

The Blood Road (Book VI)

The Carpathian Interlude Series

Immortui (Part I)

Lykoi (Part II)

Thanatos (Part III)

The Mythologia Series

Chariot of the Son

Heart of Fire: A Novel of the Ancient Olympics

Saturnalia: A Tale of Wickedness and Redemption in Ancient Rome

Titles in the Historia Non-fiction Series

Historia I: Celtic Literary Archetypes in *The Mabinogion*: A Study of the Ancient Tale of *Pwyll, Lord of Dyved*

Historia II: Arthurian Romance and the Knightly Ideal: A study of Medieval Romantic Literature and its Effect upon Warrior Culture in Europe

Historia III: *Y Gododdin*: The Last Stand of Three Hundred Britons - Understanding People and Events during Britain's Heroic Age

Historia IV: Camelot: The Historical, Archaeological and Toponymic Considerations for South Cadbury Castle as King Arthur's Capital

STAY CONNECTED

To connect with Adam and learn more about the ancient world visit www.eaglesanddragonspublishing.com

Sign up for the Eagles and Dragons Publishing Newsletter at www.eaglesanddragonspublishing.com/newsletter-join-the-legions/ to receive a FREE BOOK, first access to new releases and posts on ancient history, special offers, and much more!

Readers can also connect with Adam on Twitter @AdamHaviaras and Instagram @ adam_haviaras.

On Facebook you can 'Like' the Eagles and Dragons page to get regular updates on new historical fiction and fantasy from Eagles and Dragons Publishing.

Printed in Great Britain
by Amazon